"I want to go through your clothes."

"Oh, really?" Kirby drew out the words.

"For the painting," he explained.

"You don't want to do a nude? That's the usual line."

"I don't waste my time with lines," Adam stated. "I'm going to paint you because you were meant to be painted. I'm going to make love to you for exactly the same reason."

Kirby's expression didn't change, but her pulse rate did. "How decisive and arrogant of you," she drawled. "I haven't agreed to pose for you, Adam, nor have I agreed to sleep with you. In fact, I have serious doubts I'll do either. Shall we go?"

Before she could get to the door, he had her. His speed surprised her, though the strength didn't. She'd hoped to annoy him, but when she looked up at him she didn't see temper. She saw cool, patient determination.

Nothing could have been more unnerving.

Dear Reader,

When two people fall in love, the world is suddenly new and exciting, and it's that same excitement we bring to you in Silhouette Intimate Moments. These are stories with scope, with grandeur. These characters lead the lives we all dream of, and everything they do reflects the wonder of being in love.

Longer and more sensuous than most romances, Silhouette Intimate Moments novels take you away from everyday life and let you share the magic of love. Adventure, glamour, drama, even suspense—these are the passwords that let you into a world where love has a power beyond the ordinary, where the best authors in the field today create stories of love and commitment that will stay with you always.

In coming months look for novels by your favorite authors: Maura Seger, Parris Afton Bonds, Elizabeth Lowell and Erin St. Claire, to name just a few. And whenever you buy books, look for all the Silhouette Intimate Moments, love stories *for* today's women *by* today's women.

Leslie J. Wainger
Senior Editor
Silhouette Books

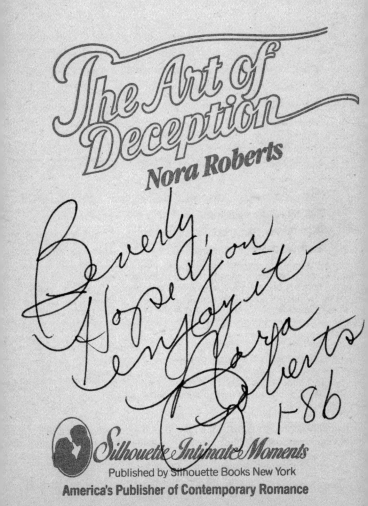

The Art of Deception

Nora Roberts

Beverly—
Hope you
enjoy it
Nora Roberts
1-86

Silhouette Intimate Moments

Published by Silhouette Books New York

America's Publisher of Contemporary Romance

SILHOUETTE BOOKS
300 E. 42nd St., New York, N.Y. 10017

ISBN: 0-373-07131-0

First Silhouette Books printing February 1986

America's Publisher of Contemporary Romance

Printed in the U.S.A.

Books by Nora Roberts

NORA ROBERTS

lives with her two sons in the Blue Ridge Mountains of western Maryland. To be a published author was her lifetime dream, which she has fulfilled in the many books that she has written for Silhouette. Renowned for her warm characters and wit, Nora Roberts is a favorite of romance readers.

For the Romance Writers of America
In gratitude for the friends I've made
and the friends still to come.

Chapter 1

It was more like a castle than a house. The stone was gray, but beveled at the edges, Herodian-style, so that it shimmered with underlying colors. Towers and turrets jutted toward the sky, joined together by a crenellated roof. Windows were mullioned, long and narrow with diamond-shaped panes.

The structure—Adam would never think of it as anything so ordinary as a house—loomed over the Hudson, audacious and eccentric and, if such things were possible, pleased with itself. If the stories were true, it suited its owner perfectly.

All it required, Adam decided as he crossed the flagstone courtyard, was a dragon and a moat.

Two grinning gargoyles sat on either side of the wide stone steps. He passed by them with a reservation natural to a practical man. Gargoyles and turrets could be accepted in their proper place—but not in rural New York a few hours' drive out of Manhattan.

Deciding to reserve judgment, he lifted the heavy brass knocker and let it fall against a door of thick Honduras mahogany. After a third pounding, the door creaked open. With strained patience, Adam looked down at a small woman with huge gray eyes, black braids and a soot-streaked face. She wore a rumpled sweatshirt and jeans that had seen better days. Lazily, she rubbed her nose with the back of her hand and stared back.

"Hullo."

He bit back a sigh, thinking that if the staff ran to half-witted maids, the next few weeks were going to be very tedious. "I'm Adam Haines. Mr. Fairchild is expecting me," he enunciated.

Her eyes narrowed with curiosity or suspicion, he couldn't be sure. "Expecting you?" Her accent was broad New England. After another moment of staring, she frowned, shrugged, then moved aside to let him in.

The hall was wide and seemingly endless. The paneling gleamed a dull deep brown in the diffused light. Streaks of sun poured out of a high angled window and fell over the small woman, but he barely noticed. Paintings. For the moment, Adam forgot the fatigue of the journey and his annoyance. He forgot everything else but the paintings.

Van Gogh, Renoir, Monet. A museum could claim no finer exhibition. The power pulled at him. The hues, the tints, the brush strokes, and the overall magnificence they combined to create, tugged at his senses. Perhaps, in some strange way, Fairchild had been right to house them in something like a fortress. Turning, Adam saw the maid with her hands loosely folded, her huge gray eyes on his face. Impatience sprang back.

"Run along will you? Tell Mr. Fairchild I'm here."

"And who might you be?" Obviously impatience didn't affect her.

"Adam Haines," he repeated. He was a man accustomed to servants—and one who expected efficiency.

"Ayah, so you said."

How could her eyes be smoky and clear at the same time, he wondered fleetingly. He gave a moment's thought to the fact that they reflected a maturity and intelligence at odds with her braids and smeared face. "Young lady..." He paced the words, slowly and distinctly. "Mr. Fairchild is expecting me. Just tell him I'm here. Can you handle that?"

A sudden dazzling smile lit her face. "Ayah."

The smile threw him off. He noticed for the first time that she had an exquisite mouth, full and sculpted. And there was something... something under the soot. Without thinking, he lifted a hand intending to brush some off. The tempest hit.

"I can't do it! I tell you it's impossible. A travesty!" A man barreled down the long curved stairs at an alarming rate. His face was shrouded in tragedy, his voice croaked with doom. "This is all your fault." Coming to a breathless stop, he pointed a long thin finger at the little maid. "It's on your head, make no mistake."

Robin Goodfellow, Adam thought instantly. The man was the picture of Puck, short with a spritely build, a face molded on cherubic lines. The spare thatch of light hair nearly stood on end. He seemed to dance. His thin legs lifted and fell on the landing as he waved the long finger at the dark-haired woman. She remained serenely undisturbed.

"Your blood pressure's rising every second, Mr. Fairchild. You'd better take a deep breath or two before you have a spell."

"Spell!" Insulted, he danced faster. His face glowed pink with the effort. "I don't have spells, girl. I've never had a spell in my life."

"There's always a first time." She nodded, keeping her fingers lightly linked. "Mr. Adam Haines is here to see you."

"Haines? What the devil does Haines have to do with it? It's the end, I tell you. The climax." He placed a hand dramatically over his heart. The pale blue eyes watered so that for one awful moment, Adam thought he'd weep. "Haines?" he repeated. Abruptly he focused on Adam with a brilliant smile. "I'm expecting you, aren't I?"

Cautiously Adam offered his hand. "Yes."

"Glad you could come, I've been looking forward to it." Still showing his teeth, he pumped Adam's hand. "Into the parlor," he said, moving his grip from Adam's hand to his arm. "We'll have a drink." He walked with the quick bouncing stride of a man who hadn't a worry in the world.

In the parlor Adam had a quick impression of antiques and old magazines. At a wave of Fairchild's hand he sat on a horsehair sofa that was remarkably uncomfortable. The maid went to an enormous stone fireplace and began to scrub out the hearth with quick tuneful little whistles.

"I'm having scotch," Fairchild decided and reached for a decanter of Chivas Regal.

"That'll be fine."

"I admire your work, Adam Haines." Fairchild offered the scotch with a steady hand. His face was calm, his voice moderate. Adam wondered if he'd imagined the scene on the stairs.

"Thank you." Sipping scotch, Adam studied the little genius across from him.

Small networks of lines crept out from Fairchild's eyes and mouth. Without them and the thinning hair, he might have been taken for a very young man. His aura of youth seemed to spring from an inner vitality, a feverish energy. The eyes were pure, unfaded blue. Adam knew they could see beyond what others saw.

Philip Fairchild was, indisputably, one of the greatest living artists of the twentieth century. His style ranged from the flamboyant to the elegant, with a touch of everything in between. For more than thirty years, he'd enjoyed a position of fame, wealth and respect in artistic and popular circles, something very few people in his profession achieved during their lifetime.

Enjoy it he did, with a temperament that ranged from pompous to irascible to generous. From time to time he invited other artists to his house on the Hudson, to spend weeks or months working, absorbing or simply relaxing. At other times, he barred everyone from the door and went into total seclusion.

"I appreciate the opportunity to work here for a few weeks, Mr. Fairchild."

"My pleasure." The artist sipped scotch and sat, gesturing with a regal wave of his hand—the king granting benediction.

Adam successfully hid a smirk. "I'm looking forward to studying some of your paintings up close. There's such incredible variety in your work."

"I live for variety," Fairchild said with a giggle. From the hearth came a distinct snort. "Disrepectful brat," Fairchild muttered into his drink. When he scowled at her, the maid tossed a braid over her shoulder and plopped her rag noisily into the bucket. "Cards!" Fairchild bellowed so suddenly Adam nearly dumped the scotch in his lap.

"I beg your pardon?"

"No need for that," Fairchild said graciously and shouted again. At the second bellow the epitome of butlers walked into the parlor.

"Yes, Mr. Fairchild." His voice was grave, lightly British. The dark suit he wore was a discreet contrast to the white hair and pale skin. He held himself like a soldier.

"See to Mr. Haines's car, Cards, and his luggage. The Wedgwood guest room."

"Very good, sir," the butler agreed after a slight nod from the woman at the hearth.

"And put his equipment in Kirby's studio," Fairchild added, grinning as the hearth scrubber choked. "Plenty of room for both of you," he told Adam before he scowled. "My daughter, you know. She's doing sculpture, up to her elbows in clay or chipping at wood and marble. I can't cope with it." Gripping his glass in both hands, Fairchild bowed his head. "God knows I try. I've put my soul into it. And for what?" he demanded, jerking his head up again. "For what?"

"I'm afraid I—"

"Failure!" Fairchild moaned, interrupting him. "To have to deal with failure at my age. It's on your head," he told the little brunette again. "You have to live with it—if you can."

Turning, she sat on the hearth, folded her legs under her and rubbed more soot on her nose. "You can hardly blame me if you have four thumbs and your soul's lost." The accent was gone. Her voice was low and smooth, hinting of European finishing schools. Adam's eyes narrowed. "You're determined to be better than I," she went on. "Therefore, you were doomed to fail before you began."

"Doomed to fail! Doomed to fail, am I?" He was up and dancing again, scotch sloshing around in his glass. "Philip Fairchild will overcome, you heartless brat. He shall triumph! You'll eat your words."

"Nonsense." Deliberately, she yawned. "You have your medium, Papa, and I have mine. Learn to live with it."

"Never." He slammed a hand against his heart again. "Defeat is a four letter word."

"Six," she corrected, and rising, commandeered the rest of his scotch.

He scowled at her, then at his empty glass. "I was speaking metaphorically."

"How clever." She kissed his cheek, transferring soot.

"Your face is filthy," Fairchild grumbled.

Lifting a brow, she ran a finger down his cheek. "So's yours."

They grinned at each other. For a flash, the resemblance was so striking, Adam wondered how he'd missed it. Kirby Fairchild, Philip's only child, a well-respected artist and eccentric in her own right. Just what, Adam wondered, was the darling of the jet set doing scrubbing out hearths?

"Come along, Adam." Kirby turned to him with a casual smile. "I'll show you to your room. You look tired. Oh, Papa," she added as she moved to the door, "this week's issue of *People* came. It's on the server. That'll keep him entertained," she said to Adam as she led him up the stairs.

He followed her slowly, noting that she walked with the faultless grace of a woman who'd been taught how to move. The pigtails swung at her back. Jeans, worn white at the stress points, had no designer label on the back pocket. Her canvas Nikes had broken shoelaces.

Kirby glided along the second floor, passing half a dozen doors before she stopped. She glanced at her hands, then at Adam. "You'd better open it. I'll get the knob filthy."

He pushed open the door and felt like he was stepping back in time. Wedgwood blue dominated the color scheme. The furniture was all Middle Georgian—carved armchairs, ornately worked tables. Again there were paintings, but this time, it was the woman behind him who held his attention.

"Why did you do that?"

"Do what?"

"Put on that act at the door." He walked back to where she stood at the threshold. Looking down, he calculated that she barely topped five feet. For the second time he had the urge to brush the soot from her face to discover what lay beneath.

"You looked so polished, and you positively glowered." She leaned a shoulder against the doorjamb. There was an elegance about him that intrigued her, because his eyes were sharp and arrogant. Though she didn't smile, the amusement in her expression was soft and ripe. "You were expecting a dim-witted parlor maid, so I made it easy for you. Cocktails at seven. Can you find your way back, or shall I come for you?"

He'd make do with that for now. "I'll find it."

"All right. *Ciao*, Adam."

Unwillingly fascinated, he watched her until she'd turned the corner at the end of the hall. Perhaps Kirby Fairchild would be as interesting a nut to crack as her father. But that was for later.

Adam closed the door and locked it. His bags were already set neatly beside the rosewood wardrobe. Taking the briefcase, Adam spun the combination lock and drew up the lid. He pulled out a small transmitter and flicked a switch.

"I'm in."

"Password," came the reply.

He swore, softly and distinctly. "Sea gull. And that is, without a doubt, the most ridiculous password on record."

"Routine, Adam. We've got to follow routine."

"Sure." There'd been nothing routine since he'd stopped his car at the end of the winding uphill drive. "I'm in, McIntyre, and I want you to know how much I appreciate your dumping me in this madhouse." With a flick of his thumb, he cut McIntyre off.

Without stopping to wash, Kirby jogged up the steps to her father's studio. She opened the door then slammed it so that jars and tubes of paint shuddered on their shelves.

"What have you done this time?" she demanded.

"I'm starting over." Wispy brows knit, he huddled over a moist lump of clay. "Fresh start. Rebirth."

"I'm not talking about your futile attempts with clay. Adam Haines," she said before he could retort. Like a small tank, she advanced on him. Years before, Kirby had learned size was of no consequence if you had a knack for intimidation. She'd developed it meticulously. Slamming her palms down on his work table, she stood nose to nose with him. "What the hell do you mean by asking him here and not even telling me?"

"Now, now, Kirby." Fairchild hadn't lived six decades without knowing when to dodge and weave. "It simply slipped my mind."

Better than anyone else, Kirby knew nothing slipped his mind. "What're you up to now, Papa?"

"Up to?" He smiled guilelessly.

"Why did you ask him here now, of all times?"

"I've admired his work. So've you," he pointed out when her mouth thinned. "He wrote such a nice letter about *Scarlet Moon* when it was exhibited at the Metropolitan last month."

Her brow lifted, an elegant movement under a layer of soot. "You don't invite everyone who compliments your work."

"Of course not, my sweet. That would be impossible. One must be . . . selective. Now I must get back to my work while the mood's flowing."

"Something's going to flow," she promised. "Papa, if you've a new scheme after you promised—"

"Kirby!" His round, smooth face quivered with emotion. His lips trembled. It was only one of his talents. "You'd doubt the word of your own father? The seed that spawned you?"

"That makes me sound like a gardenia, and it won't work." She crossed her arms over her chest. Frowning, Fairchild poked at the unformed clay.

"My motives are completely altruistic."

"Hah."

"Adam Haines is a brilliant young artist. You've said so yourself."

"Yes, he is, and I'm sure he'd be delightful company under different circumstances." She leaned forward, grabbing her father's chin in her hand. "Not now."

"Ungracious," Fairchild said with disapproval. "Your mother, rest her soul, would be very disappointed in you."

Kirby ground her teeth. "Papa, the Van Gogh!"

"Coming along nicely," he assured her. "Just a few more days."

Knowing she was in danger of tearing out her hair, she stalked to the tower window. "Oh, bloody murder."

Senility, she decided. It had to be senility. How could he consider having that man here now? Next week, next month, but now? That man, Kirby thought ruthlessly, was nobody's fool.

At first glance she'd decided he wasn't just attractive—very attractive—but sharp. Those big camel's eyes gleamed with intelligence. The long, thin mouth equaled determination. Perhaps he was a bit pompous in his bearing and manner, but he wasn't soft. No, she was certain instinctively that Adam Haines would be hard as nails.

She'd like to do him in bronze, she mused. The straight nose, the sharp angles and planes in his face. His hair was nearly the color of deep, polished bronze and just a tad too long for convention. She'd want to capture his air of arrogance and authority. But not now!

Sighing, she moved her shoulders. Behind her back, Fairchild grinned. When she turned back to him, he was studiously intent on his clay.

"He'll want to come up here, you know." Despite the soot, she dipped her hands in her pockets. They had a problem; now it had to be dealt with. For the better part of her life, Kirby had sorted through the confusion her father gleefully created. The truth was, she'd have had it no other way. "It would seem odd if we didn't show him your studio."

"We'll show him tomorrow."

"He mustn't see the Van Gogh." Kirby planted her feet, prepared to do battle on this one point if not the others. "You're not going to make this more complicated than you already have."

"He won't see it. Why should he?" Fairchild glanced up briefly, eyes wide. "It has nothing to do with him."

Though she realized it was foolish, Kirby was reassured. No, he wouldn't see it, she thought. Her father might be a little . . . unique, she decided, but he wasn't careless. Neither was she. "Thank God it's nearly finished."

"Another few days and off it goes, high into the mountains of South America." He made a vague, sweeping gesture with his hands.

Moving over, Kirby uncovered the canvas that stood on an easel in the far corner. She studied it as an artist, as a lover of art and as a daughter.

The pastoral scene wasn't peaceful but vibrant. The brush strokes were jagged, almost fierce, so that the simple setting had a frenzied kind of motion. No, it didn't sit still waiting for admiration. It reached out and grabbed by the throat. It spoke of pain, of triumph, of agonies and joys. Her lips tilted because she had no choice. Van Gogh, she knew, could have done no better.

"Papa." When she turned her head, their eyes met in perfect understanding. "You are incomparable."

By seven, Kirby had not only resigned herself to their house guest, but was prepared to enjoy him. It was a basic trait of her character to enjoy what she had to put up with. As she poured vermouth into a glass, she realized she was looking forward to seeing him again, and to getting beneath the surface gloss. She had a feeling there might be some fascinating layers in Adam Haines.

She dropped into a high-backed chair, crossed her legs and tuned back in to her father's rantings.

"It hates me, fails me at every turn. Why, Kirby?" He spread his hands in an impassioned plea. "I'm a good man, loving father, faithful friend."

"It's your attitude, Papa." She shrugged a shoulder as she drank. "Your emotional plane's faulty."

"There's nothing wrong with my emotional plane." Sniffing, Fairchild lifted his glass. "Not a damn thing wrong with it. It's the clay that's the problem, not me."

"You're cocky," she said simply. Fairchild made a sound like a train straining up a long hill.

"Cocky? *Cocky?* What the devil kind of word is that?"

"Adjective. Two syllables, five letters."

Adam heard the byplay as he walked toward the parlor. After a peaceful afternoon, he wondered if he were ready to cope with another bout of madness. Fairchild's voice was rising steadily, and as Adam paused in the doorway, he saw that the artist was up and shuffling again.

McIntyre was going to pay for this, Adam decided. He'd see to it that revenge was slow and thorough. When Fairchild pointed an accusing finger, Adam followed its direction. For an instant he was totally and uncharacteristically stunned.

The woman in the chair was so completely removed from the grimy, pigtailed chimney sweep, he found it nearly impossible to associate the two. She wore a thin silk dress as dark as her hair, draped at the bodice and slit up the side to show off one smooth thigh. He studied her profile as she watched her father rant. It was gently molded, classically oval with a very subtle sweep of cheekbones. Her lips were full, curved now in just a hint of a smile. Without the soot, her skin was somewhere between gold and honey with a look of luxurious softness. Only the eyes reminded him this was the same woman—gray and large and amused. Lifting one hand, she tossed back the dark hair that covered her shoulders.

There was something more than beauty here. Adam knew he'd seen women with more beauty than Kirby Fairchild. But there was something... He groped for the word, but it eluded him.

As if sensing him, she turned—just her head. Again she stared at him, openly and with curiosity as her father continued his ravings. Slowly, very slowly, she smiled. Adam felt the power slam into him.

Sex, he realized abruptly. Kirby Fairchild exuded sex the way other women exuded perfume. Raw, unapologetic sex.

With a quick assessment typical of him, Adam decided she wouldn't be easy to deceive. However he handled Fairchild, he'd have to tred carefully with Fairchild's daughter. He decided as well that he already wanted to make love to her. He'd have to tred *very* carefully.

"Adam." She spoke in a soft voice that nonetheless carried over her father's shouting. "You seem to have found us. Come in, Papa's nearly done."

"Done? I'm undone. And by my own child." Fairchild moved toward Adam as he entered the room. "Cocky, she says. I ask you, is that a word for a daughter to use?"

"An aperitif?" Kirby asked. She rose with a fluid motion that Adam had always associated with tall, willowy women.

"Yes, thank you."

"Your room's agreeable?" His face wreathed in smiles again, Fairchild plopped down on the sofa.

"Very agreeable." The best way to handle it, Adam decided, was to pretend everything was normal. Pretenses were, after all, part of the game. "You have an...exceptional house."

"I'm fond of it." Content, Fairchild leaned back. "It was built near the turn of the century by a wealthy and insane English lord. You'll take Adam on a tour tomorrow, won't you, Kirby?"

"Of course." As she handed Adam a glass, she smiled into his eyes. Diamonds, cold as ice, glittered at her ears. He could feel the heat rise.

"I'm looking forward to it." Style, he concluded. Whether natural or developed, Miss Fairchild had style.

She smiled over the rim of her own glass, thinking precisely the same thing about Adam. "We aim to please."

A cautious man, Adam turned to Fairchild again. "Your art collection rivals a museum's. The Titian in my room is fabulous."

The Titian, Kirby thought in quick panic. How could she have forgotten it? What in God's name could she do about it? No difference. It made no difference, she reassured herself. It couldn't, because there was nothing to be done.

"The Hudson scene on the west wall—" Adam turned to her just as Kirby was telling herself to relax "—is that your work?"

"My... Oh, yes." She smiled as she remembered. She'd deal with the Titian at the first opportunity. "I'd forgotten that. It's sentimental, I'm afraid. I was home from school and had a crush on the chauffeur's son. We used to neck down there."

"He had buck teeth," Fairchild reminded her with a snort.

"Love conquers all," Kirby decided.

"The Hudson riverbank is a hell of a place to lose your virginity," her father stated, suddenly severe. He swirled his drink, then downed it.

Enjoying the abrupt paternal disapproval, she decided to poke at it. "I didn't lose my virginity on the Hudson riverbank." Amusement glimmered in her eyes. "I lost it in a Renault in Paris."

Love conquers all, Adam repeated silently.

"Dinner is served," Cards announced with dignity from the doorway.

"And about time, too." Fairchild leaped up. "A man could starve in his own home."

With a smile at her father's retreating back, Kirby offered Adam her hand. "Shall we go in?"

In the dining room, Fairchild's paintings dominated. An enormous Waterford chandelier showered light over mahogany and crystal. A massive stone fireplace thundered with flame and light. There were scents of burning wood, candles and roasted meat. There was Breton lace and silver. Still, his paintings dominated.

It appeared he had no distinct style. Art was his style, whether he depicted a sprawling light-filled landscape or a gentle, shadowy portrait. Bold brush strokes or delicate ones, oils streaked on with a pallet knife or misty watercolors, he'd done them all. Magnificently.

As varied as his paintings were his opinions on other artists. While they sat at the long, laden table, Fairchild spoke of each artist personally, as if he'd been

transported back in time and had developed relation-
ships with Raphael, Goya, Manet.

His theories were intriguing, his knowledge impressive. The artist in Adam responded to him. The practical part, the part that had come to do a job,
remained cautious. The opposing forces made him
uncomfortable. His attraction to the woman across
from him made him itchy.

He cursed McIntyre.

Adam decided the weeks with the Fairchilds might
be interesting despite their eccentricities. He didn't
care for the complications, but he'd allowed himself
to be pulled in. For now, he'd sit back and observe,
waiting for the time to act.

The information he had on them was sketchy. Fairchild was just past sixty, a widower of nearly twenty
years. His art and his talent were no secrets, but his
personal life was veiled. Perhaps due to temperament. Perhaps, Adam mused, due to necessity.

About Kirby, he knew almost nothing. Professionally, she'd kept a low profile until her first showing the
year before. Though it had been an unprecedented
success, both she and her father rarely sought publicity on their work. Personally, she was often written up
in the glossies and tabloids as she jetted to Saint
Moritz with this year's tennis champion or to Martin-
ique with the current Hollywood golden boy. He knew
she was twenty-seven and unmarried. Not for lack of
opportunity, he concluded. She was the type of woman men would constantly pursue. In another century,
duels would have been fought over her. Adam thought
she'd have enjoyed the melodrama.

From their viewpoint, the Fairchilds knew of Adam only what was public knowledge. He'd been born under comfortable circumstances, giving him both the time and means to develop his talent. At the age of twenty, his reputation as an artist had begun to take root. A dozen years later, he was well established. He'd lived in Paris, then in Switzerland before settling back in the States.

Still, during his twenties, he'd traveled often while painting. With Adam, his art had always come first. However, under the poised exterior, under the practicality and sophistication, there was a taste for adventure and a streak of cunning. So there had been McIntyre.

He'd just have to learn control, Adam told himself as he thought of McIntyre. He'd just have to learn how to say no, absolutely no. The next time Mac had an inspiration, he could go to hell with it.

When they settled back in the parlor with coffee and brandy, Adam calculated that he could finish the job in a couple of weeks. True, the place was immense, but there were only a handful of people in it. After his tour he'd know his way around well enough. Then it would be routine.

Satisfied, he concentrated on Kirby. At the moment she was the perfect hostess—charming, personable. All class and sophistication. She was, momentarily, precisely the type of woman who'd always appealed to him—well-groomed, well-mannered, intelligent, lovely. The room smelled of hothouse roses, wood smoke and her own tenuous scent, which seemed to blend the two. Adam began to relax with it.

"Why don't you play, Kirby?" Fairchild poured a second brandy for himself and Adam. "It helps clear my mind."

"All right." With a quick smile for Adam, Kirby moved to the far end of the room, running a finger over a wing-shaped instrument he'd taken for a small piano.

It took only a few notes for him to realize he'd been wrong. A harpsichord, he thought, astonished. The tinny music floated up. Bach. Adam recognized the composer and wondered if he'd fallen down the rabbit hole. No one—no one normal—played Bach on a harpsichord in a castle in the twentieth century.

Fairchild sat, his eyes half closed, one thin finger tapping while Kirby continued to play. Her eyes were grave, her mouth faintly moist and sober. Suddenly, without missing a note or moving another muscle, she sent Adam a slow wink. The notes flowed into Brahms. In that instant, Adam knew he was not only going to take her to bed. He was going to paint her.

"I've got it!" Fairchild leaped up and scrambled around the room. "I've got it. Inspiration. The golden light!"

"Amen," Kirby murmured.

"I'll show you, you wicked child." Grinning like one of his gargoyles, Fairchild leaned over the harpsichord. "By the end of the week, I'll have a piece that'll make anything you've ever done look like a doorstop."

Kirby raised her brows and kissed him on the mouth. "Goat droppings."

"You'll eat your words," he warned as he dashed out of the room.

"I sincerely hope not." Rising, she picked up her drink. "Papa has a nasty competitive streak." Which constantly pleased her. "More brandy?"

"Your father has a . . . unique personality." An emerald flashed on her hand as she filled her glass again. He saw her hands were narrow, delicate against the hard glitter of the stone. But there'd be strength in them, he reminded himself as he moved to the bar to join her. Strength was indispensible to an artist.

"You're diplomatic." She turned and looked up at him. There was the faintest hint of rose on her lips. "You're a very diplomatic person, aren't you, Adam?"

He'd already learned not to trust the nunlike expression. "Under some circumstances."

"Under most circumstances. Too bad."

"Is it?"

Because she enjoyed personal contact during any kind of confrontation, she kept her eyes on his while she drank. Her irises were the purest gray he'd ever seen, with no hint of other colors. "I think you'd be a very interesting man if you didn't bind yourself up. I believe you think everything through very carefully."

"You see that as a problem?" His voice had cooled. "It's a remarkable observation after such a short time."

No, he wouldn't be a bore, she decided, pleased with his annoyance. It was lack of emotion Kirby found tedious. "I could've come by it easily enough after an hour, but I'd already seen your work. Besides talent, you have self-control, dignity and a strong sense of the conventional."

"Why do I feel as though I've been insulted?"

"Perceptive, too." She smiled, that slow curving of lips that was fascinating to watch. When he answered it, she made up her mind quickly. She'd always found it the best way. Still watching him, she set down her brandy. "I'm impulsive," she explained. "I want to see what it feels like."

Her arms were around him, her lips on his in a move that caught him completely off balance. He had a very brief impression of wood smoke and roses, of incredible softness and strength, before she drew back. The hint of a smile remained as she picked up her brandy and finished it off. She'd enjoyed the brief kiss, but she'd enjoyed shocking him a great deal more.

"Very nice," she said with borderline approval. "Breakfast is from seven on. Just ring for Cards if you need anything. Good night."

She turned to leave, but he took her arm. Kirby found herself whirled around. When their bodies collided, the surprise was hers.

"You caught me off guard," he said softly. "I can do much better than nice."

He took her mouth swiftly, molding her to him. Soft to hard, thin silk to crisp linen. There was something primitive in her taste, something...ageless. She brought to his mind the woods on an autumn evening—dark, pungent and full of small mysteries.

The kiss lengthened, deepened without plan on either side. Her response was instant, as her responses often were. It was boundless as they often were. She moved her hands from his shoulders, to his neck, to his face, as if she were already sculpting. Something vibrated between them.

For the moment, blood ruled. She was accustomed to it; he wasn't. He was accustomed to reason, but he found none here. Here was heat and passion, needs and desires without questions or answers.

Ultimately, reluctantly, he drew back. Caution, because he was used to winning, was his way.

She could still taste him. Kirby wondered, as she felt his breath feather over her lips, how she'd misjudged him. Her head was spinning, something new for her. She understood heated blood, a fast pulse, but not the clouding of her mind.

Not certain how long he'd have the advantage, Adam smiled at her. "Better?"

"Yes." She waited until the floor became solid under her feet again. "That was quite an improvement." Like her father, she knew when to dodge and weave. She eased herself away and moved to the doorway. She'd have to do some thinking, and some re-evaluating. "How long are you here, Adam?"

"Four weeks," he told her, finding it odd she didn't know.

"Do you intend to sleep with me before you go?"

Torn between amusement and admiration, he stared at her. He respected candor, but he wasn't used to it in quite so blunt a form. In this case, he decided to follow suit. "Yes."

She nodded, ignoring the little thrill that raced up her spine. Games—she liked to play them. To win them. Kirby sensed one was just beginning between her and Adam. "I'll have to think about that, won't I? Good night."

Chapter 2

Shafts of morning light streamed in the long windows of the dining room and tossed their diamond pattern on the floor. Outside the trees were touched with September. Leaves blushed from salmon to crimson, the colors mixed with golds and rusts and the last stubborn greens. The lawn was alive with fall flowers and shrubs that seemed caught on fire. Adam had his back to the view as he studied Fairchild's paintings.

Again, Adam was struck with the incredible variety of styles Fairchild cultivated. There was a still life with the light and shadows of a Goya, a landscape with the frantic colors of a Van Gogh, a portrait with the sensitivity and grace of a Raphael. Because of its subject, it was the portrait that drew him.

A frail, dark-haired woman looked out from the canvas. There was an air of serenity, of patience about her. The eyes were the same pure gray as Kirby's but the features were gentler, more even. Kirby's mother had been a rare beauty, a rare woman who looked like she'd had both strength and understanding. While she wouldn't have scrubbed at a hearth, she would have understood the daughter who did. That Adam could see this, be certain of it, without ever having met Rachel Fairchild, was only proof of Fairchild's genius. He created life with oil and brush.

The next painting, executed in the style of Gainsborough, was a full-length portrait of a young girl. Glossy black curls fell over the shoulders of a white muslin dress, tucked at the bodice, belled at the skirt. She wore white stockings and neat black buckle shoes. Touches of color came from the wide pink sash around her waist and the dusky roses she carried in a basket. But this was no demure *Pinky*.

The girl held her head high, tilting it with youthful arrogance. The half smile spoke of devilment while the huge gray eyes danced with both. No more than eleven or twelve, Adam calculated. Even then Kirby must have been a handful.

"An adorable child, isn't she?" Kirby stood at the doorway as she had for five full minutes. She'd enjoyed watching and dissecting him as much as Adam had enjoyed dissecting the painting.

He stood very straight—prep school training, Kirby decided. Yet his hands were dipped comfortably in his pockets. Even in a casual sweater and jeans, there was an air of formality about him. Contrasts intrigued her, as a woman and as an artist.

Turning, Adam studied her as meticulously as he had her portrait. The day before he'd seen her go from grubby urchin to sleek sophisticate. Today she was the picture of the bohemian artist. Her face was free of cosmetics and unframed as her hair hung in a pony-tail down her back. She wore a shapeless black sweater, baggy, paint-streaked jeans and no shoes. To his annoyance, she continued to attract him.

She turned her head, and by accident or design, the sunlight fell over her profile. In that instant, she was breathtaking. Kirby sighed as she studied her own face. "A veritable angel."

"Apparently her father knew better."

She laughed, low and rich. His calm, dry voice pleased her enormously. "He did at that, but not everyone sees it." She was glad he had, simply be-cause she appreciated a sharp eye and a clever mind. "Have you had breakfast?"

He relaxed. She'd turned again so that the light no longer illuminated her face. She was just an attrac-tive, friendly woman. "No, I've been busy being awed."

"Oh, well, one should never be awed on an empty stomach. It's murder on the digestion." After press-ing a button, she linked her arm through his and led him to the table. "After we've eaten I'll take you through the house."

"I'd like that." Adam took the seat opposite her. She wore no fragrance this morning but soap—clean and sexless. It aroused nonetheless.

A woman clumped into the room. She had a long bony face, small mud-brown eyes and an unfortunate nose. Her graying hair was scraped back and bundled at the nape of her neck. The deep furrows in her brow indicated her pessimistic nature. Glancing over, Kirby smiled.

"Good morning, Tulip. You'll have to send a tray up to Papa, he won't budge out of the tower." She drew a linen napkin from its ring. "Just toast and coffee for me, and don't lecture. I'm not getting any taller."

After a grumbling disapproval, Tulip turned to Adam. His order of bacon and eggs received the same grumble before she clumped back out again.

"Tulip?" Adam cocked a brow as he turned to Kirby.

"Fits beautifully, doesn't it?" Lips sober, eyes amused, she propped her elbows on the table and dropped her face in her hands. "She's really a marvel as far as organizing. We've had a running battle over food for fifteen years. Tulip insists that if I eat, I'll grow. After I hit twenty, I figured I'd proved her wrong. I wonder why adults insist on making such absurd statements to children."

The robust young maid who'd served dinner the night before brought in coffee. She showered sunbeam smiles over Adam.

"Thank you, Polly." Kirby's voice was gentle, but Adam caught the warning glance and the maid's quick blush.

"Yes, ma'am." Without a backward glance, Polly scurried from the room. Kirby poured the coffee herself.

"Our Polly is very sweet," she began. "But she has a habit of becoming, ah, a bit too matey with two-thirds of the male population." Setting down the silver coffee urn, Kirby smiled across the table. "If you've a taste for slap and tickle, Polly's your girl. Otherwise, I wouldn't encourage her. I've even had to warn her off Papa.''

The picture of the lusty young Polly with the puck-like Fairchild zipped into Adam's mind. It lingered there a moment with perfect clarity until he roared with laughter.

Well, well, well, Kirby mused, watching him. A man who could laugh like that had tremendous potential. She wondered what other surprises he had tucked away. Hopefully she'd discover quite a few during his stay.

Picking up the cream pitcher, he added a stream to his coffee. "You have my word, I'll resist temptation.''

"She's built stupendously," Kirby observed as she sipped her coffee black.

"Really?" It was the first time she'd seen his grin—quick, crooked and wicked. "I hadn't noticed.''

Kirby studied him while the grin did odd things to her nervous system. Surprise again, she told herself, then reached for her coffee. "I've misjudged you, Adam," she murmured. "A definite miscalculation. You're not precisely what you seem.''

He thought of the small transmitter locked in his dignified briefcase. "Is anyone?"

"Yes." She gave him a long and completely guile-less look. "Yes, some people are precisely what they seem, for better or worse.''

"You?" He asked because he suddenly wanted to know badly who and what she was. Not for McIntyre, not for the job, but for himself.

She was silent a moment as a quick, ironic smile moved over her face. He guessed, correctly, that she was laughing at herself. "What I seem to be today is what I am—today." With one of her lightning changes, she threw off the mood. "Here's breakfast."

They talked a little as they ate, inconsequential things, polite things that two relative strangers speak about over a meal. They'd both been raised to handle such situations—small talk, intelligent give and take that skimmed over the surface and meant absolutely nothing.

But Kirby found herself aware of him, more aware than she should have been. More aware than she wanted to be.

Just what kind of man was he, she wondered as he sprinkled salt on his eggs. She'd already concluded he wasn't nearly as conventional as he appeared to be— or perhaps as he thought himself. There was an adventurer in there, she was certain. Her only annoyance stemmed from the fact that it had taken her so long to see it.

She remembered the strength and turbulence of the kiss they'd shared. He'd be a demanding lover. And a fascinating one. Which meant she'd have to be a great deal more careful. She no longer believed he'd be easily managed. Something in his eyes . . .

Quickly she backed off from that line of thought. The point was she had to manage him. Finishing off her coffee she sent up a quick prayer that her father had the Van Gogh well concealed.

"The tour begins from bottom to top," she said brightly. Rising, she held out her hand. "The dungeons are marvelously morbid and damp, but I think we'll postpone that in respect of your cashmere sweater.''

"Dungeons?" He accepted her offered arm and walked from the room with her.

"We don't use them now, I'm afraid, but if the vibrations are right, you can still hear a few moans and rattles." She said it so casually, he nearly believed her. That, he realized, was one of her biggest talents. Making the ridiculous sound plausible. "Lord Wickerton, the original owner, was quite dastardly."

"You approve?"

"Approve?" She weighed this as they walked. "Perhaps not, but it's easy to be intrigued by things that happened nearly a hundred years ago. Evil can become romantic after a certain period of time, don't you think?"

"I've never looked at it quite that way."

"That's because you have a very firm grip on what's right and what's wrong."

He stopped, and because their arms were linked, Kirby stopped beside him. He looked down at her with an intensity that put her on guard. "And you?"

She opened her mouth, then closed it again before she could say something foolish. "Let's just say I'm flexible. You'll enjoy this room," she said, pushing open a door. "It's rather sturdy and staid."

Taking the insult in stride, Adam walked through with her. For nearly an hour they wandered from room to room. It occurred to him that he'd underestimated the sheer size of the place. Halls snaked and angled, rooms popped up where they were least expected, some tiny, some enormous. Unless he got very, very lucky, Adam concluded, the job would take him a great deal of time.

Pushing open two heavy, carved doors, Kirby led him into the library. It had two levels and was the size of an average two-bedroom apartment. Faded Persian rugs were scattered over the floor. The far wall was glassed in the small diamond panes that graced most of the windows in the house. The rest of the walls were lined floor to ceiling with books. A glance showed Chaucer standing beside D.H. Lawrence. Steven King leaned against Milton. There wasn't even the pretense of organization, but there was the rich smell of leather, dust and lemon oil.

The books dominated the room and left no space for paintings. But there was sculpture.

Adam crossed the room and lifted a figure of a stallion carved in walnut. Freedom, grace, movement, seemed to vibrate in his hands. He could almost hear the steady heartbeat against his palm.

There was a bronze bust of Fairchild on a high, round stand. The artist had captured the puckishness, the energy; but more, she'd captured a gentleness and generosity Adam had yet to see.

In silence, he wandered the room, examining each piece as Kirby looked on. He made her nervous and she struggled against it. Nerves were something she felt rarely, and never acknowledged. Her work had been looked at before, she reminded herself. What else did an artist want but recognition? She linked her fingers and remained silent. His opinion hardly mattered, she told herself, then moistened her lips.

He picked up a piece of marble shaped into a roaring mass of flames. Though the marble was white, the fire was real. Like every other piece he'd examined, the mass of marble flames was physical. Kirby had inherited her father's gift for creating life.

For a moment Adam forgot all the reasons he was there and thought only of the woman and the artist. "Where did you study?"

The flip remark she'd been prepared to make vanished from her mind the moment he turned and looked at her with those calm brown eyes. "École des Beaux Arts formally. But Papa taught me always."

He turned the marble in his hands. Even a pedestrian imagination would've felt the heat. Adam could all but smell it. "How long have you been sculpting?"

"Seriously? About four years."

"Why the hell have you only had one exhibition? Why are you burying it here?"

Anger. She lifted her brow at it. She'd wondered just what sort of a temper he'd have, but she hadn't expected to see it break through over her work. "I'm having another in the spring," she said evenly. "Charles Larson's handling it." Abruptly uncomfortable, she shrugged. "Actually I was pressured into having the other. I wasn't ready."

"That's ridiculous." He held up the marble as if she hadn't seen it before. "Absolutely ridiculous."

Why should it make her feel vulnerable to have her work in the palm of his hand? Turning away, Kirby ran a finger down her father's bronze nose. "I wasn't ready," she repeated, not sure why, when she never explained herself to anyone, she was explaining such things to him. "I had to be sure, you see. There are those who say—who'll always say—that I rode on

Papa's coattails. That's to be expected." She blew out a breath but her hand remained on the bust of her father. "I had to know differently. *I* had to know."

He hadn't expected sensitivity, sweetness, vulnerability. Not from her. But he'd seen it in her work, and he'd heard it in her voice. It moved him, every bit as much as her passion had. "Now you do."

She turned again, and her chin tilted. "Now I do." With an odd smile she crossed over and took the marble from him. "I've never told anyone that before— not even Papa." When she looked up her eyes were quiet, soft and curious. "I wonder why it should be you."

He touched her hair, something he'd wanted to do since he'd seen the morning sun slant on it. "I wonder why I'm glad it was."

She took a step back. There was no ignoring a longing so quick and so strong. There was no forgetting caution. "Well, we'll have to think about it, I suppose. This concludes the first part of our tour." She set the marble down and smiled easily, "All comments and questions are welcome."

He'd dipped below the surface, Adam realized, and she didn't care for it. That he understood. "Your home's...overwhelming," he decided and made her smile broaden into a grin. "I'm disappointed there isn't a moat and dragon."

"Just try leaving your vegetables on your plate and you'll see what a dragon Tulip can be. As to the moat..." She started to shrug an apology, then remembered. "Toadstools, how could I have forgotten!"

Without waiting for an answer, she grabbed his hand and dashed back to the parlor. "No moat," she told him as she went directly to the fireplace. "But there are secret passageways."

"I should've known."

"It's been quite a while since I—" She broke off and began to mutter to herself as she pushed and tugged at the carved oak mantel. "I swear it's one of the flowers along here—there's a button, but you have to catch it just right." With an annoyed gesture, she flicked the ponytail back over her shoulder. Adam watched her long, elegant fingers push and prod. He saw her nails were short, rounded and unpainted. A schoolgirl's nails, or a nun's. Yet the impression of sexual vitality remained. "I know it's here, but I can't quite... *Et voilà*." Pleased with herself, Kirby stepped back as a section of paneling slid creakily aside. "Needs some oil," she decided.

"Impressive," Adam murmured, already wondering if his luck had come in. "Does it lead to the dungeons?"

"It spreads out all over the house in a maze of twists and turns." Moving to the entrance with him, she peered into the dark. "There's an entrance in nearly every room. A button on the other side opens or closes the panel. The passages are horribly dark and moldy." With a shudder, she stepped back. "Perhaps that's why I forgot about them." Suddenly cold, she rubbed her hands together. "I used to haunt them as a child, drove the servants mad."

"I can imagine." But he saw the quick dread in her eyes as she looked back into the dark.

"I paid for it, I suppose. One day my flashlight went out on me and I couldn't find my way out. There're spiders down there as big as schnauzers." She laughed, but took another step back. "I don't know how long I was in there, but when Papa found me I was hysterical. Needless to say, I found other ways to terrorize the staff."

"It still frightens you."

She glanced up, prepared to brush it off. For the second time the quiet look in his eyes had her telling the simple truth. "Yes. Yes, apparently it does. Well, now that I've confessed my neurosis, let's move on."

The panel closed, grumbling in protest as she pushed the control. Adam felt rather than heard her sigh of relief. When he took her hand he found it cold. He wanted to warm it, and her. Instead he concentrated on just what the passages could mean to him. With them he'd have access to every room without the risk of running into one of the staff or one of the Fairchilds. When an opportunity was tossed in your lap, you took it for what it was worth. He'd begin tonight.

"A delivery for you, Miss Fairchild."

Both Kirby and Adam paused on the bottom landing of the stairs. Kirby eyed the long white box the butler held in his hands. "Not again, Cards."

"It would appear so, miss."

"Galoshes." Kirby sniffed, scratched a point just under her jaw and studied the box. "I'll just have to be more firm."

"Just as you say, miss."

"Cards . . ." She smiled at him, and though his face remained inscrutable, Adam would have sworn he came to attention. "I know it's rude, but give them to Polly. I can't bear to look at another red rose."

"As you wish, miss. And the card?"

"Details," she muttered, then sighed. "Leave it on my desk, I'll deal with it. Sorry, Adam." Turning, she started up the stairs again. "I've been bombarded with roses for the last three weeks. I've refused to become Jared's mistress, but he's persistent." More exasperated than annoyed, she shook her head as they rounded the first curve. "I suppose I'll have to threaten to tell his wife."

"Might work," Adam murmured.

"I ask you, shouldn't a man know better by the time he hits sixty?" Rolling her eyes, she bounced up the next three steps. "I can't imagine what he's thinking of."

She smelled of soap and was shapeless in the sweater and jeans. Moving behind her to the second story, Adam could imagine very well.

The second floor was lined with bedrooms. Each was unique, each furnished in a different style. The more Adam saw of the house, the more he was charmed. And the more he realized how complicated his task was going to be.

"The last room, my boudoir." She gave him the slow, lazy smile that made his palms itchy. "I'll promise not to compromise you as long as you're aware my promises aren't known for being kept." With a light laugh, she pushed open the door and stepped inside. "Fish fins."

"I beg your pardon?"

"Whatever for?" Ignoring him, Kirby marched into the room. "Do you see that?" she demanded. In a gesture remarkably like her father's she pointed at the bed. A scruffy dog lay like a lump in the center of a wedding ring quilt. Frowning, Adam walked a little closer.

"What is it?"

"A dog, of course."

He looked at the gray ball of hair that seemed to have no front or back. "It's possible."

A stubby tail began to thump on the quilt.

"This is no laughing matter, Montique. I take the heat, you know."

Adam watched the bundle shift until he could make out a head. The eyes were still hidden behind the mop of fur, but there was a little black nose and a lolling tongue. "Somehow I'd've pictured you with a brace of Afghan hounds."

"What? Oh." Giving the mop on the bed a quick pat, she turned back to Adam. "Montique doesn't belong to me, he belongs to Isabelle." She sent the dog an annoyed glance. "She's going to be very put out."

Adam frowned at the unfamiliar name. Had McIntyre missed someone? "Is she one of the staff?"

"Good grief, no." Kirby let out a peal of laughter that had Montique squirming in delight. "Isabelle serves no one. She's... Well, here she is now. There'll be the devil to pay," she added under her breath.

Shifting his head, Adam looked toward the doorway. He started to tell Kirby there was no one there when a movement caught his eye. He looked down on a large buff-colored Siamese. Her eyes were angled, icily blue, and though he hadn't considered such things before, regally annoyed. The cat crossed the threshold, sat and stared up at Kirby.

"Don't look at me like that," Kirby tossed out. "I had nothing to do with it. If he wanders in here, it has nothing to do with me." Isabelle flicked her tail and made a low, dangerous sound in her throat. "I won't tolerate your threats, and I will not keep my door locked." Kirby folded her arms and tapped a foot on the Aubusson carpet. "I refuse to change a habit of a lifetime for your convenience. You'll just have to keep a closer eye on him."

As he watched silently, Adam was certain he saw genuine temper in Kirby's eyes—the kind of temper one person aims toward another person. Gently he placed a hand on her arm and waited for her to look at him. "Kirby, you're arguing with a cat."

"Adam." Just as gently, she patted his hand. "Don't worry. I can handle it." With a lift of her brow, she turned back to Isabelle. "Take him, then, and put him on a leash if you don't want him wandering. And the next time, I'd appreciate it if you'd knock before you come into my room."

With a flick of her tail, Isabelle moved to the bed and stared up at Montique. He thumped his tail, tongue lolling before he leaped clumsily to the floor. With a kind of jiggling trot, he followed the gliding cat from the room.

"He went with her," Adam murmured.

"Of course he did," Kirby retorted. "She has a beastly temper."

Refusing to be taken for a fool, Adam gave Kirby a long, uncompromising look. "Are you trying to tell me that the dog belongs to that cat?"

"Do you have a cigarette?" she countered. "I rarely smoke, but Isabelle affects me that way." She noted that his eyes never lost their cool, mildly annoyed expression as he took one out and lit it for her. Kirby had to swallow a chuckle. Adam was, she decided, remarkable. She drew on the cigarette and blew out the smoke without inhaling. "Isabelle maintains that Montique followed her home. I think she kidnapped him. It would be just like her."

Games, he thought again. Two could play. "And to whom does Isabelle belong?"

"Belong?" Kirby's eyes widened. "Isabelle belongs to no one but herself. Who'd want to lay claim to such a wicked creature?"

And he could play as well as anyone. Taking the cigarette from her, Adam drew in smoke. "If you dislike her, why don't you just get rid of her?"

She nipped the cigarette from his fingers again. "I can hardly do that as long as she pays the rent, can I? There that's enough," she decided after another drag. "I'm quite calm again." She handed him back the cigarette before she walked to the door. "I'll take you up to Papa's studio. We'll just skip over the third floor, everything's draped with dustcovers."

Adam opened his mouth then decided that some things were best left alone. Dismissing odd cats and ugly dogs, he followed Kirby back into the hall again. The stairs continued up in a lazy arch to the third floor, then veered sharply and became straight and narrow. Kirby stopped at the transition point and gestured down the hall.

"The floor plan is the same as the second floor. There's a set of stairs at the opposite side that lead to my studio. The rest of these rooms are rarely used."

She gave him the slow smile as she linked hands. "Of course, the entire floor's haunted."

"Of course." He found it only natural. Without a word, he followed her to the tower.

Chapter 3

Normalcy. Tubes of paint were scattered everywhere, brushes stood in jars. The scent of oil and turpentine hung in the air. This Adam understood—the debris and the sensuality of art.

The room was rounded with arching windows and a lofty ceiling. The floor might have been beautiful at one time, but now the wood was dull and splattered and smeared with paints and stains. Canvases were in the corners, against the walls, stacked on the floor.

Kirby gave the room a swift, thorough study. When she saw all was as it should be, the tension eased from her shoulders. Moving across the room, she went to her father.

He sat, motionless and unblinking, staring down at a partially formed mound of clay. Without speaking, Kirby walked around the work table, scrutinizing the clay from all angles. Fairchild's eyes remained riveted on his work. After a few moments, Kirby straightened, rubbed her nose with the back of her hand and pursed her lips.

"Mmm."

"That's only your opinion," Fairchild snapped.

"It certainly is." For a moment she nibbled on her thumbnail. "You're entitled to another. Adam, come have a look."

He sent her a killing glance that caused her to grin. Trapped by manners, he crossed the studio and looked down at the clay.

It was, he supposed, an adequate attempt—a partially formed hawk, talons exposed, beak just parted. The power, the life that sung in his paints, and in his daughter's sculptures, just wasn't there. In vain, Adam searched for a way out.

"Hmm," he began, only to have Kirby pounce on the syllable.

"There, he agrees with me." Kirby patted her father's head and looked smug.

"What does he know?" Fairchild demanded. "He's a painter."

"And so, darling Papa, are you. A brilliant one."

He struggled not to be pleased and poked a finger into the clay. "Soon, you hateful brat, I'll be a brilliant sculptor as well."

"I'll get you some Play-Doh for your birthday," she offered, then let out a shriek as Fairchild grabbed her ear and twisted. "Fiend." With a sniff she rubbed at the lobe.

"Mind your tongue or I'll make a Van Gogh of you."

As Adam watched, the little man cackled; Kirby, however, froze—face, shoulders, hands. The fluidity he'd noticed in her even when she was still, vanished. It wasn't annoyance, he thought, but . . . fear? Not of Fairchild. Kirby, he was certain, would never be afraid of a man, particularly her father. *For* Fairchild was more feasible, and just as baffling.

She recovered quickly enough and tilted her chin. "I'm going to show Adam my studio. He can settle in."

"Good, good." Because he recognized the edge to her voice, Fairchild patted her hand. "Damn pretty girl, isn't she, Adam?"

"Yes, she is."

As Kirby heaved a gusty sigh, Fairchild patted her hand again. The clay on his smeared onto hers. "See, my sweet, aren't you grateful for those braces now?"

"Papa." With a reluctant grin, Kirby lay her cheek against his balding head. "I never wore braces."

"Of course not. You inherited your teeth from me." He gave Adam a flashing smile and a wink. "Come back when you've got settled, Adam. I need some masculine company." He pinched Kirby's cheek lightly. "And don't think Adam's going to sniff around your ankles like Rick Potts."

"Adam's nothing like Rick," Kirby murmured as she picked up a rag and wiped the traces of clay from her hands. "Rick is sweet."

"She inherited her manners from the milkman," Fairchild observed.

She shot a look at Adam. "I'm sure Adam can be sweet, too." But there was no confidence in her voice. "Rick's forte is watercolor. He's the sort of man women want to mother. I'm afraid he stutters a bit when he gets excited.''

''He's madly in love with our little Kirby.'' Fairchild would've cackled again but for the look his daughter sent him.

''He just thinks he is. I don't encourage him.''

''What about the clinch I happened in on in the library?'' Pleased with himself, Fairchild turned back to Adam. ''I ask you, when a man's glasses are steamed, isn't there a reason for it?''

''Invariably.'' He liked them, damn it, whether they were harmless lunatics or something more than harmless. He liked them both.

''You know very well that was totally one-sided.'' Barely shifting her stance, she became suddenly regal and dignified. ''Rick lost control, temporarily. Like blowing a fuse, I suppose.'' She brushed at the sleeve of her sweater. ''Now that's quite enough on the subject.''

''He's coming to stay for a few days next week.'' Fairchild dropped the bombshell as Kirby walked to the door. To her credit, she barely broke stride. Adam wondered if he were watching a well-plotted game of chess or a wild version of Chinese checkers.

''Very well,'' Kirby said coolly. ''I'll tell Rick that Adam and I are lovers and that Adam's viciously jealous, and keeps a stiletto in his left sock.''

''Good God,'' Adam murmured as Kirby swept out of the door. ''She'll do it, too.''

''You can bank on it,'' Fairchild agreed without disguising the glee in his voice. He loved confusion. A man of sixty was entitled to create as much as he possibly could.

The structure of the second tower studio was identical to the first. Only the contents differed. In addition to paints and brushes and canvases, there were knives, chisels and mallets. There were slabs of limestone and marble and lumps of wood. Adam's equipment was the only spot of order in the room. Cards had stacked his gear personally.

A long wooden table was cluttered with tools, wood shavings, rags and a crumpled ball of material that might've been a paint smock. In a corner was a high-tech stereo component system. An ancient gas heater was set into one wall with an empty easel in front of it.

As with Fairchild's tower, Adam understood this kind of chaos. The room was drenched with sun. It was quiet, spacious and instantly appealing.

"There's plenty of room," Kirby told him with a sweeping gesture. "Set up where you're comfortable. I don't imagine we'll get in each other's way," she said doubtfully, then shrugged. She had to make the best of it. Better he were here, in her way, than sharing her father's studio with the Van Gogh. "Are you temperamental?"

"I wouldn't say so," Adam answered absently as he began to unpack his equipment. "Others might. And you?"

"Oh, yes." Kirby plopped down behind the work table and lifted a piece of wood. "I have tantrums and fits of melancholia. I hope it won't bother you." He turned to answer, but she was staring down at the wood in her hands, as if searching for something hidden inside. "I'm doing my emotions now. I can't be held responsible."

Curious, Adam left his unpacking to walk to the shelf behind her. On it were a dozen pieces in various stages. He chose a carved piece of fruitwood that had been polished. "Emotions," he murmured, running his fingers over the wood.

"Yes, that's—"

"*Grief*," he supplied. He could see the anguish, feel the pain.

"Yes." She wasn't sure if it pleased her or not to have him so in tune—particularly with that one piece that had cost her so much. "I've done *Joy* and *Doubt* as well. I thought to save *Passion* for last." She spread her hands under the wood she held and brought it to eye level. "This is to be *Anger*." As if to annoy it, she tapped the wood with her fingers. "One of the seven deadly sins, though I've always thought it mislabeled. We need anger."

He saw the change in her eyes as she stared into the wood. Secrets, he thought. She was riddled with them. Yet as she sat, the sun pouring around her, the un-formed wood held aloft in her hands, she seemed to be utterly, utterly open, completely readable, washed with emotion. Even as he began to see it, she shifted and broke the mood. Her smile when she looked up at him was teasing.

"Since I'm doing *Anger*, you'll have to tolerate a few bouts of temper."

"I'll try to be objective."

Kirby grinned, liking the gloss of politeness over the sarcasm. "I bet you have bundles of objectivity."

"No more than my share."

"You can have mine, too, if you like. It's very small." Still moving the wood in her hands, she glanced toward his equipment. "Are you working on anything?"

"I was." He walked around to stand in front of her. "I've something else in mind now. I want to paint you."

Her gaze shifted from the wood in her hands to his face. With some puzzlement, he saw her eyes were wary. "Why?"

He took a step closer and closed his hand over her chin. Kirby sat passively as he examined her from different angles. But she felt his fingers, each individual finger, as it lay on her skin. Soft skin, and Adam didn't bother to resist the urge to run his thumb over her cheek. The bones seemed fragile under his hands, but her eyes were steady and direct.

"Because," he said at length, "your face is fascinating. I want to paint that, the translucence, and your sexuality."

Her mouth heated under the careless brush of his fingers. Her hands tightened on the fruitwood, but her voice was even. "And if I said no?"

That was another thing that intrigued him, the trace of hauteur she used sparingly—and very successfully. She'd bring men to their knees with that look, he thought. Deliberately he leaned over and kissed her. He felt her stiffen, resist, then remain still. She was, in her own way, in her own defense, absorbing the feelings he brought to her. Her knuckles had whitened on the wood, but he didn't see. When he lifted his head, all Adam saw was the deep, pure gray of her eyes.

"I'd paint you anyway," he murmured. He left the room, giving them both time to think about it.

She did think about it. For nearly thirty minutes Kirby sat perfectly still and let her mind work. It was a curious part of her nature that such a vibrant, restless woman could have such a capacity for stillness. When it was necessary, Kirby could do absolutely nothing while she thought through problems and looked for answers. Adam made it necessary.

He stirred something in her that she'd never felt before. Kirby believed that one of the most precious things in life was the original and the fresh. This time, however, she wondered if she should skirt around it.

She appreciated a man who took the satisfaction of his own desires for granted, just as she did. Nor was she adverse to pitting herself against him. But . . . She couldn't quite get past the *but* in Adam's case.

It might be safer—smarter, she amended—if she concentrated on the awkwardness of Adam's presence with respect to the Van Gogh and her father's hobby. The attraction she felt was ill-timed. She touched her tongue to her top lip and thought she could taste him. Ill-timed, she thought again. And inconvenient.

Her father had better be prudent, she thought, then immediately sighed. Calling Philip Fairchild prudent was like calling Huck Finn studious. The blasted, brilliant Van Gogh was going to have to make a speedy exit. And the Titian, she remembered, gnawing on her lip. She still had to handle that.

Adam was huddled with her father, and there was nothing she could do at the moment. Just a few more days, she reminded herself. There'd be nothing more to worry about. The smile crept back to her mouth.

The rest of Adam's visit might be fun. She thought of him, the serious brown eyes, the strong, sober mouth.

Dangerous fun, she conceded. But then, what was life without a bit of danger? Still smiling, she picked up her tools.

She worked in silence, in total concentration. Adam, her father, the Van Gogh were forgotten. The wood in her hand was the center of the universe. There was life there; she could feel it. It only waited for her to find the key to release it. She would find it, and the soaring satisfaction that went hand in hand with the discovery.

Painting had never given her that. She'd played at it, enjoyed it, but she'd never possessed it. She'd never been possessed by it. Art was a lover that demanded complete allegiance. Kirby understood that.

As she worked, the wood seemed to take a tentative breath. She felt suddenly, clearly, the temper she sought push against the confinement. Nearly—nearly free.

At the sound of her name, she jerked her head up. "Bloody murder!"

"Kirby, I'm so sorry."

"Melanie." She swallowed the abuse, barely. "I didn't hear you come up." Though she set down her tools, she continued to hold the wood. She couldn't lose it now. "Come in. I won't shout at you."

"I'm sure you should." Melanie hesitated at the doorway. "I'm disturbing you."

"Yes, you are, but I forgive you. How was New York?" Kirby gestured to a chair as she smiled at her oldest friend.

Pale blond hair was elegantly styled around a heart-shaped face. Cheekbones, more prominent than Kirby's, were tinted expertly. The Cupid's bow mouth was carefully glossed in deep rose. Kirby decided, as she did regularly, that Melanie Burgess had the most perfect profile ever created.

"You look wonderful, Melly. Did you have fun?"

Melanie wrinkled her nose as she brushed off the seat of her chair. "Business. But my spring designs were well received."

Kirby brought up her legs and crossed them under her. "I'll never understand how you can decide in August what we should be wearing next April." She was losing the power of the wood. Telling herself it would come back, she set it on the table, within reach. "Have you done something nasty to the hemlines again?"

"You never pay any attention anyway." She gave Kirby's sweater a look of despair.

"I like to think of my wardrobe as timeless rather than trendy." She grinned knowing which buttons to push. "This sweater's barely twelve years old."

"And looks every day of it." Knowing the game and Kirby's skill, Melanie switched tactics. "I ran into Ellen Parker at Twenty-one."

"Did you?" After lacing her hands, Kirby rested her chin on them. She never considered gossiping rude, particularly if it was interesting. "I haven't seen her for months. Is she still spouting French when she wants to be confidential?"

"You won't believe it." Melanie shuddered as she pulled a long, slender cigarette from an enameled case. "I didn't believe it myself until I saw it with my own eyes. Jerry told me. You remember Jerry Turner, don't you?''

"Designs women's underwear."

"Intimate apparel," Melanie corrected with a sigh. "Really, Kirby."

"Whatever. I appreciate nice underwear. So what did he tell you?"

Melanie pulled out a monogrammed lighter and flicked it on. She took a delicate puff. "He told me that Ellen was having an affair."

"There's news," Kirby returned dryly. With a yawn she stretched her arms to the ceiling and relieved the stiffness in her shoulder blades. "Is this number two hundred and three, or have I missed one?"

"But, Kirby—" Melanie tapped her cigarette for emphasis as she leaned forward "—she's having this one with her son's orthodontist."

It was the sound of Kirby's laughter that caused Adam to pause on his way up the tower steps. It rang against the stone walls, rich, real and arousing. He stood as it echoed and faded. Moving quietly, he continued up.

"Kirby, really. An orthodontist." Even knowing Kirby as well as she did, Melanie was stunned by her reaction. "It's so—so middle class."

"Oh, Melanie, you're such a wonderful snob." She smothered another chuckle as Melanie gave an indignant huff. When Kirby smiled, it was irresistible. "It's perfectly acceptable for Ellen to have any number of affairs, as long as she keeps her choice socially prominent but an orthodontist goes beyond good taste?"

"It's not acceptable, of course," Melanie muttered, finding herself caught in the trap of Kirby's logic. "But if one is discreet, and..."

"Selective?" Kirby supplied good-naturedly. "Actually it is rather nasty. Here's Ellen carrying on with her son's orthodontist while poor Harold shells out a fortune for the kid's overbite. Where's the justice?"

"You say the most astonishing things."

"Orthodonture work is frightfully expensive."

With an exasperated sigh, Melanie tried another change of subject. "How's Stuart?"

Though he'd been about to enter, Adam stopped in the doorway and kept his silence. Kirby's smile had vanished. The eyes that had been alive with humor were frigid. Something hard, strong and unpleasant came into them. Seeing the change, Adam realized she'd make a formidable enemy. There was grit behind the careless wit, the raw sexuality and the eccentric rich-girl polish. He wouldn't forget it.

"Stuart," Kirby said in a brittle voice. "I really wouldn't know."

"Oh dear." At the arctic tone, Melanie caught her bottom lip between her teeth. "Have you two had a row?"

"A row?" The smile remained unpleasant. "One might put it that way." Something flared—the temper she'd been prodding out of the wood. With an effort, Kirby shrugged it aside. "As soon as I'd agreed to marry him, I knew I'd made a mistake. I should've dealt with it right away."

"You'd told me you were having doubts." After stubbing out her cigarette, Melanie leaned forward to take Kirby's hands. "I thought it was nerves. You'd never let any relationship get as far as an engagement before."

"It was an error in judgment." No, she'd never let a relationship get as far as an engagement. Engagements equaled commitment. Commitments were a lock, perhaps the only lock, Kirby considered sacred. "I corrected it."

"And Stuart? I suppose he was furious."

The smile that came back to Kirby's lips held no humor. "He gave me the perfect escape hatch. You know he'd been pressuring me to set a date?"

"And I know that you'd been putting him off."

"Thank God," Kirby murmured. "In any case, I'd finally drummed up the courage to renege. I think it was the first time in my life I've felt genuine guilt." Moving her shoulders restlessly, she picked up the wood again. It helped to steady her, helped her to concentrate on temper. "I went by his place, unannounced. It was a now or never sort of gesture. I should've seen what was up as soon as he answered the door, but I was already into my neat little speech when I noticed a few—let's say articles of intimate apparel tossed around the room.

"Oh, Kirby."

Letting out a long breath, Kirby went on. "That part of it was my fault, I suppose. I wouldn't sleep with him. There was just no driving urge to be intimate with him. No..." She searched for a word. "Heat," she decided for lack of anything better. "I guess that's why I knew I'd never marry him. But, I was faithful." The fury whipped through her again. "I was faithful, Melly."

"I don't know what to say." Distress vibrated in her voice. "I'm so sorry, Kirby."

Kirby shook her head at the sympathy. She never looked for it. "I wouldn't have been so angry if he hadn't stood there, telling me how much he loved me when he had another woman keeping the sheets warm. I found it humiliating."

"You have nothing to be humiliated about," Melanie returned with some heat. "He was a fool."

"Perhaps. It would've been bad enough if we'd stuck to the point, but we got off the track of love and fidelity. Things got nasty."

Her voice trailed off. Her eyes clouded over. It was time for secrets again. "I found out quite a bit that night," she murmured. "I've never thought of myself as a fool, but it seems I'd been one."

Again, Melanie reached for her hand. "It must have been a dreadful shock to learn Stuart was unfaithful even before you were married."

"What?" Blinking, Kirby brought herself back. "Oh, that. Yes, that, too."

"Too? What else?"

"Nothing." With a shake of her head, Kirby swept it all aside. "It's all dead and buried now."

"I feel terrible. Damn it, I introduced you."

"Perhaps you should shave your head in restitution, but I'd advise you to forget it."

"Can you?"

Kirby's lips curved up, her brow lifted. "Tell me, Melly, do you still hold André Fayette against me?"

Melanie folded her hands primly. "It's been five years."

"Six, but who's counting?" Grinning, Kirby leaned forward. "Besides, who expects an oversexed French art student to have any taste?"

Melanie's pretty mouth pouted. "He was very attractive."

"But base." Kirby struggled with a new grin. "No class, Melly. You should thank me for luring him away, however unintentionally."

Deciding it was time to make his presence known, Adam stepped inside. Kirby glanced up and smiled without a trace of the ice or the fury. "Hello, Adam. Did you have a nice chat with Papa?"

"Yes."

Melanie, he decided as he glanced in her direction, was even more stunning at close quarters. Classic face, classic figure draped in a pale rose dress cut with style and simplicity. "Am I interrupting?"

"Just gossip. Melanie Burgess, Adam Haines. Adam's our guest for a few weeks."

Adam accepted the slim rose-tipped hand. It was soft and pampered, without the slight ridge of callus that Kirby's had just under the fingers. He wondered what had happened in the past twenty-four hours to make him prefer the untidy artist to the perfectly groomed woman smiling up at him. Maybe he was coming down with something.

"*The* Adam Haines?" Melanie's smile warmed. She knew of him, the irreproachable lineage and education. "Of course you are," she continued before he could comment. "This place attracts artists like a magnet. I have one of your paintings."

"Do you?" Adam lit her cigarette then one of his own. "Which one?"

"*A Study in Blue.*" Melanie tilted her face to smile into his eyes, a neat little feminine trick she'd learned soon after she'd learned to walk.

From across the table, Kirby studied them both. Two extraordinary faces, she decided. The tips of her fingers itched to capture Adam in bronze. A year before she'd done Melanie in ivory—smooth, cool and perfect. With Adam, she'd strive for the undercurrents.

"I wanted the painting because it was so strong," Melanie continued. "But I nearly let it go because it made me sad. You remember, Kirby. You were there."

"Yes, I remember." When she looked up at him her eyes were candid and amused, without the traces of flirtation that flitted in Melanie's. "I was afraid she'd break down and disgrace herself so I threatened to buy it myself. Papa was furious that I didn't."

"Uncle Philip could practically stock the Louvre already," Melanie said with a casual shrug.

"Some people collect stamps," Kirby returned, then smiled again. "The still life in my room is Melanie's work, Adam. We studied together in France."

"No, don't ask," Melanie said quickly, holding up her hand. "I'm not an artist. I'm a designer who dabbles."

"Only because you refuse to dig your toes in."

Melanie inclined her head, but didn't agree or refute. "I must go. Tell Uncle Philip I said hello. I won't risk disturbing him as well."

"Stay for lunch, Melly. We haven't seen you in two months."

"Another time." She rose with the grace of one who'd been taught to sit and stand and walk. Adam stood with her, catching the drift of Chanel. "I'll see you this weekend at the party." With another smile, she offered Adam her hand. "You'll come, too, won't you?"

"I'd like that."

"Wonderful." Snapping open her bag, Melanie drew out thin leather gloves. "Nine o'clock, Kirby. Don't forget. Oh!" On her way to the door, she stopped, whirling back. "Oh, God, the invitations were sent out before I . . . Kirby, Stuart's going to be there."

"I won't pack my derringer, Melly." She laughed, but it wasn't quite as rich or quite as free. "You look as though someone's just spilled caviar on your St. Laurent. Don't worry about it." She paused, and the chill passed quickly in and out of her eyes. "I promise you, I won't."

"If you're sure . . ." Melanie frowned. It was, however, not possible to discuss such a thing in depth in front of a guest. "As long as you won't be uncomfortable."

"I won't be the one who suffers discomfort." The careless arrogance was back.

"Saturday, then." Melanie gave Adam a final smile before she slipped from the room.

"A beautiful woman," Adam commented, coming back to the table.

"Yes, exceptional." The simple agreement had no undertones of envy or spite.

"How do two women, two exceptional women, of totally different types, remain friends?"

"By not attempting to change one another." She picked up the wood again and began to roll it around in her hands. "I overlook what I see as Melanie's faults, and she overlooks mine." She saw the pad and pencil in his hand and lifted a brow. "What're you doing?"

"Some preliminary sketches. What are your faults?"

"Too numerous to mention." Setting the wood down again, she leaned back.

"Any good points?"

"Dozens." Perhaps it was time to test him a bit, to see what button worked what switch. "Loyalty," she began breezily. "Sporadic patience and honesty."

"Sporadic?"

"I'd hate to be perfect." She ran her tongue over her teeth. "And I'm terrific in bed."

His gaze shifted to her bland smile. Just what game was Kirby Fairchild playing? His lips curved as easily as hers. "I bet you are."

Laughing, she leaned forward again, chin cupped in her hands. "You don't rattle easily, Adam. It makes me all the more determined to keep trying."

"Telling me something I'd already concluded isn't likely to rattle me. Who's Stuart?"

The question had her stiffening. She'd challenged him, Kirby conceded, now she had to meet one of his. "A former fiancé," she said evenly. "Stuart Hiller."

The name clicked, but Adam continued to sketch. "The same Hiller who runs the Merrick Gallery?"

"The same." He heard the tightening in her voice. For a moment he wanted to drop it, to leave her to her privacy and her anger. The job came first.

"I know him by reputation," Adam continued. "I'd planned to see the gallery. It's about twenty miles from here, isn't it?"

She paled a bit, which confused him, but when she spoke her voice was steady. "Yes, it's not far. Under the circumstances, I'm afraid I can't take you."

"You may mend your differences over the weekend." Prying wasn't his style. He had a distaste for it, particularly when it involved someone he was beginning to care about. When he lifted his gaze, however, he didn't see discomfort. She was livid.

"I think not." She made a conscious effort to relax her hands. Noting the gesture, Adam wondered how much it cost her. "It occurred to me that my name would be Fairchild-Hiller." She gave a slow, rolling shrug. "That would never do."

"The Merrick Gallery has quite a reputation."

"Yes. As a matter of fact, Melanie's mother owns it, and managed it until a couple of years ago."

"Melanie? Didn't you say her name was Burgess?"

"She was married to Carlyse Burgess—Burgess Enterprises. They're divorced."

"So, she's Harriet Merrick's daughter." The cast of players was increasing. "Mrs. Merrick's given the running of the gallery over to Hiller?"

"For the most part. She dips her hand in now and then."

Adam saw that she'd relaxed again and concentrated on the shape of her eyes. Round? Not quite, he decided. They were nearly almond shaped, but again, not quite. Like Kirby, they were simply unique.

"Whatever my personal feelings, Stuart's a knowledgeable dealer." She gave a quick, short laugh.

"Since she hired him, she's had time to travel. Harriet's just back from an African safari. When I phoned her the other day, she told me she'd brought back a necklace of crocodile teeth."

To his credit, Adam closed his eyes only briefly. "Your families are close then. I imagine your father's done a lot of dealing through the Merrick Gallery."

"Over the years. Papa had his first exhibition there more than thirty years ago. It sort of lifted his and Harriet's careers off at the same time." Straightening in her chair, Kirby frowned across the table. "Let me see what you've done."

"In a minute," he muttered, ignoring her outstretched hand.

"Your manners sink to my level when it's convenient, I see." Kirby plopped back in her chair. When he didn't comment, she screwed her face into unnatural lines.

"I wouldn't do that for long," Adam advised. "You'll hurt yourself. When I start in oil, you'll have to behave or I'll beat you."

Kirby relaxed her face because her jaw was stiffening. "Corkscrews, you wouldn't beat me. You have the disadvantage of being a gentleman, inside and out."

Lifting his head, he pinned her with a look. "Don't bank on it."

The look alone stopped whatever sassy rejoinder she might have made. It wasn't the look of a gentleman, but of a man who made his own way however he chose. Before she could think of a proper response, the sound of shouting and wailing drifted up the tower steps and through the open door. Kirby made no move to spring up and investigate. She merely smiled.

"I'm going to ask two questions," Adam decided. "First, what the hell is that?"

"Which that is that, Adam?" Her eyes were dove gray and guileless.

"The sound of mourning."

"Oh, that." Grinning, she reached over and snatched his sketch pad. "That's Papa's latest tantrum because his sculpture's not going well—which of course it never will. Does my nose really tilt that way?" Experimentally she ran her finger down it. "Yes, I guess it does. What was your other question?"

"Why do you say 'corkscrews' or something equally ridiculous when a simple 'hell' or 'damn' would do?"

"It has to do with cigars. You really must show these sketches to Papa. He'll want to see them."

"Cigars." Determined to have her full attention, Adam grabbed the pad away from her.

"Those big, nasty fat ones. Papa used to smoke them by the carload. You needed a gas mask just to come in the door. I begged, threatened, even tried smoking them myself." She swallowed on that unfortunate memory. "Then I came up with the solution. Papa is a sucker."

"Is that so?"

"That is, he just can't resist a bet, no matter what the odds." She touched the wood again, knowing she'd have to come back to it later. "My language was, let's say, colorful. I can swear eloquently in seven languages."

"Quite an accomplishment."

"It has its uses, believe me. I bet Papa ten thousand dollars that I could go longer without swearing than he could without smoking. Both my language and the ozone layer have been clean for three months." Rising, Kirby circled the table. "I have the gratitude of the entire staff." Abruptly she dropped in his lap. Letting her head fall back, she wound her arms around his neck. "Kiss me again, will you? I can't resist."

There can't be another like her, Adam thought as he closed his mouth over hers. With a low sound of pleasure, Kirby melted against him, all soft demand.

Then neither of them thought, but felt only.

Desire was swift and sharp. It built and expanded so that they could wallow in it. She allowed herself the luxury, for such things were too often brief, too often hollow. She wanted the speed, the heat, the current. A risk, but life was nothing without them. A challenge, but each day brought its own. He made her feel soft, giddy, senseless. No one else had. If she could be swept away, why shouldn't she be? It had never happened before.

She needed what she never realized she'd needed from a man before: strength, solidity.

Adam felt the initial stir turn to an ache—something deep and dull and constant. It wasn't something he could resist, but something he found he needed. Desire had always been basic and simple and painless. Hadn't he known she was a woman who would make a man suffer? Knowing it, shouldn't he have been able to avoid it? But he hurt. Holding her soft and pliant in his arms, he hurt. From wanting more.

"Can't you two wait until after lunch?" Fairchild demanded from the doorway.

With a quiet sigh, Kirby drew her lips from Adam's. The taste lingered as she knew now it would. Like the wood behind her, it would be something that pulled her back again and again.

"We're coming," she murmured, then brushed Adam's mouth again as if in promise. She turned and rested her cheek against his in a gesture he found impossibly sweet. "Adam's been sketching me," she told her father.

"Yes, I can see that." Fairchild gave a quick snort. "He can sketch you all he chooses after lunch. I'm hungry."

Chapter 4

Food seemed to soothe Fairchild's temperament. As he plowed his way through poached salmon he went off on a long, technical diatribe on surrealism. It appeared breaking conventional thought to release the imagination had appealed to him to the extent that he'd given nearly a year of his time in study and application. With a good-humored shrug he confessed that his attempts at surrealistic painting had been poor, and his plunge into abstract little better.

"He's banished those canvases to the attic," Kirby told Adam as she poked at her salad. "There's one in shades of blue and yellow, with clocks of all sizes and shapes sort of melting and drooping everywhere and two left shoes tucked in a corner. He called it *Absence of Time*."

"Experimental," Fairchild grumbled, eyeing Kirby's uneaten portion of fish.

"He refused an obscene amount of money for it and locked it, like a mad relation, in the attic." Smoothly she transferred her fish to her father's plate. "He'll be sending his sculpture to join it before long."

Fairchild swallowed a bite of fish, then ground his teeth. "Heartless brat." In the blink of an eye he changed from amiable cherub to gnome. "By this time next year, Philip Fairchild's name will be synonymous with sculpture."

"Horse dust," Kirby concluded and speared a cucumber. "That shade of pink becomes you, Papa." Leaning over, she placed a loud kiss on his cheek. "It's very close to fuchsia."

"You're not too old to forget my ability to bring out the same tone on your bottom."

"Child abuser." As Adam watched she stood and wrapped her arms around Fairchild's neck. In the matter of love for her father, the enigma of Kirby Fairchild was easily solvable. "I'm going out for a walk before I turn yellow and dry up. Will you come?"

"No, no, I've a little project to finish." He patted her hand as she tensed. Adam saw something pass between them before Fairchild turned to him. "Take her for a walk and get on with your...sketching," he said with a cackle. "Have you asked Kirby if you can paint her yet? They all do." He stabbed at the salmon again. "She never lets them."

Adam lifted his wine. "I told Kirby I was going to paint her."

The new cackle was full of delight. Pale blue eyes lit with the pleasure of trouble brewing. "A firm hand, eh? She's always needed one. Don't know where she got such a miserable temper." He smiled artlessly. "Must've come from her mother's side."

Adam glanced up at the serene, mild-eyed woman in the portrait. "Undoubtedly."

"See that painting there?" Fairchild pointed to the portrait of Kirby as a girl. "That's the one and only time she modeled for me. I had to pay the brat scale." He gave a huff and a puff before he attacked the fish again. "Twelve years old and already mercenary."

"If you're going to discuss me as if I weren't here, I'll go fetch my shoes." Without a backward glance, Kirby glided from the room.

"Hasn't changed much, has she?" Adam commented as he drained his wine.

"Not a damn bit," Fairchild agreed proudly. "She'll lead you a merry chase, Adam, my boy. I hope you're in condition."

"I ran track in college."

Fairchild's laugh was infectious. Damn it, Adam thought again, I like him. It complicated things. From the other room he heard Kirby in a heated discussion with Isabelle. He was beginning to realize complication was the lady's middle name. What should've been a very simple job was developing layers he didn't care for.

"Come on, Adam." Kirby poked her head around the doorway. "I've told Isabelle she can come, but she and Montique have to keep a distance of five yards at all times. Papa—" she tossed her ponytail back "—I really think we ought to try raising the rent. She might look for an apartment in town."

"We should never have agreed to a long-term lease," Fairchild grumbled, then gave his full attention to Kirby's salmon.

Deciding not to comment, Adam rose and went outside.

It was warm for September and breezy. The grounds around the house were alive with fall. Beds of zinnias and mums spread out helter-skelter, flowing over their borders and adding a tang to the air. Near a flaming maple, Adam saw an old man in patched overalls. With a whimsical lack of dedication, he raked at the scattered leaves. As they neared him, he grinned toothlessly.

"You'll never get them all, Jamie."

He made a faint wheezing sound that must've been a laugh. "Sooner or later, missy. There be plenty of time."

"I'll help you tomorrow."

"Ayah, and you'll be piling them up and jumping in 'em like always." He wheezed again and rubbed a frail hand over his chin. "Stick to your whittling and could be I'll leave a pile for you."

With her hands hooked in her back pockets she scuffed at a leaf. "A nice big one?"

"Could be. If you're a good girl."

"There's always a catch." Grabbing Adam's hand, she pulled him away.

"Is that little old man responsible for the grounds?" Three acres, he calculated. Three acres if it was a foot.

"Since he retired."

"Retired?"

"Jamie retired when he was sixty-five. That was before I was born." The breeze blew strands of hair into her face and she pushed at them. "He claims to be ninety-two, but of course he's ninety-five and won't admit it." She shook her head. "Vanity."

Kirby pulled him along until they stood at a dizzying height above the river. Far below, the ribbon of water seemed still. Small dots of houses were scattered along the view. There was a splash of hues rather than distinct tones, a melding of textures.

On the ridge where they stood there was only wind, river and sky. Kirby threw her head back. She looked primitive, wild, invincible. Turning, he looked at the house. It looked the same.

"Why do you stay here?" Blunt questions weren't typical of him. Kirby had already changed that.

"I have my family, my home, my work."

"And isolation."

Her shoulders moved. Though her lashes were lowered, her eyes weren't closed. "People come here; that's not isolation."

"Don't you want to travel? To see Florence, Rome, Venice?"

From her stance on a rock, she was nearly eye level with him. When she turned to him it was without her usual arrogance. "I'd been to Europe five times before I was twelve. I spent four years in Paris on my own when I was studying."

She looked over his shoulder a moment, at nothing or at everything, he couldn't be sure. "I slept with a Breton count in a chateau, skied in the Swiss Alps and hiked the moors in Cornwall. I've traveled, and I'll travel again. But..." He knew she looked at the house now, because her lips curved. "I always come home."

"What brings you back?"

"Papa." She stopped and smiled fully. "Memories, familiarity. Insanity."

"You love him very much." She could make things impossibly complicated or perfectly simple. The job he'd come to do was becoming more and more of a burden.

"More than anything or anyone." She spoke quietly, so that her voice seemed a part of the breeze. "He's given me everything of importance: security, independence, loyalty, friendship, love—and the capability to give them back. I'd like to think someday I'll find someone who wants that from me. My home would be with him then."

How could he resist the sweetness, the simplicity she could show so unexpectedly? It wasn't in the script, he reminded himself, but reached a hand to her face, just to touch. When she brought her hand to his, something stirred in him that wasn't desire, but was just as potent.

She felt the strength in him, and sensed a confusion that might have been equal to her own. Another time, she thought. Another time it might have worked. But now, just now, there were too many other things. Deliberately she dropped her hand and turned back to the river. "I don't know why I tell you these things," she murmured. "It's not in character. Do people usually let you in on their personal thoughts?"

"No. Or maybe I haven't been listening."

She smiled and in one of her lightning changes of mood, leaped from the rock. "You're not the type people would confide in." Casually she linked her arm through his. "Though you seem to have strong, sturdy shoulders. You're a little aloof," she decided. "And just a tad pompous."

"Pompous?" How could she allure him one instant and infuriate him the next? "What do you mean, pompous?"

Because he sounded dangerously like her father, she swallowed. "Just a tad," she reminded him, nearly choking on a laugh. "Don't be offended, Adam. Pomposity certainly has its place in the world." When he continued to scowl down at her she cleared her throat of another laugh. "I like the way your left brow lifts when you're annoyed."

"I'm not pompous." He spoke very precisely and watched her lips tremble with fresh amusement.

"Perhaps that was a bad choice of words."

"It was a completely incorrect choice." Just barely he caught himself before his brow lifted. Damn the woman, he thought and swore he wouldn't smile.

"Conventional." Kirby patted his cheek. "I'm sure that's what I meant."

"I'm sure those two words mean the same thing to you. I won't be categorized by either."

Tilting her head, she studied him. "Maybe I'm wrong," she said to herself as much as him. "I've been wrong before. Give me a piggyback ride."

"*What?*"

"A piggyback ride," Kirby repeated.

"You're crazy." She might be sharp, she might be talented, he'd already conceded that, but part of her brain was permanently on holiday.

With a shrug, she started back toward the house. "I knew you wouldn't. Pompous people never give or receive piggyback rides. It's the law."

"Damn." She was doing it to him, and he was letting her. For a moment he stuck his hands in his pockets and stood firm. Let her play her games with her father, Adam told himself. He wasn't biting. With another oath, he caught up to her. "You're an exasperating woman."

"Why, thank you."

They stared at each other, him in frustration, her in amusement until he turned his back. "Get on."

"If you insist." Nimbly she jumped on his back, blew the hair out of her eyes and looked down. "Wombats, you're tall."

"You're short," he corrected and hitched her to a more comfortable position.

"I'm going to be five-seven in my next life."

"You'd better add pounds as well as inches to your fantasy." Her hands were light on his shoulders, her thighs firm around his waist. Ridiculous, he thought. Ridiculous to want her now when she's making a fool of both of you. "What do you weigh?"

"An even hundred." She sent a careless wave to Jamie.

"And when you take the ball bearings out of your pocket?"

"Ninety-six, if you want to be technical." With a laugh, she gave him a quick hug. Her laughter was warm and distracting at his ear. "You might do something daring, like not wearing socks."

"The next spontaneous act might be dropping you on your very attractive bottom."

"Is it attractive?" Idly she swung her feet back and forth. "I see so little of it myself." She held him for a moment longer because it felt so right, so good. Keep it light, she reminded herself. And watch your step. As long as she could keep him off balance, things would run smoothly. Leaning forward, she caught the lobe of his ear between her teeth. "Thanks for the lift, sailor."

Before he could respond, she'd jumped down and dashed into the house.

It was night, late, dark and quiet when Adam sat alone in his room. He held the transmitter in his hand and found he wanted to smash it into little pieces and forget it had ever existed. No personal involvements. That was rule number one and he'd always followed it. He'd never been tempted not to.

He'd wanted to follow it this time, he reminded himself. It just wasn't working that way. Involvement, emotion, conscience; he couldn't let any of it interfere. Staring at Kirby's painting of the Hudson, he flicked the switch.

"McIntyre?"

"Password."

"Damn it, this isn't a chapter of Ian Fleming."

"Procedure," McIntyre reminded him briskly. After twenty seconds of dead air, he relented. "Okay, okay, what've you found out?"

I've found out I'm becoming dangerously close to being crazy about a woman who makes absolutely no sense to me, he thought. "I've found out that the next time you have a brainstorm, you can go to hell with it."

"Trouble?" McIntyre's voice snapped into the receiver. "You were supposed to call in if there was trouble."

"The trouble is I like the old man and the daughter's . . . unsettling." An apt word, Adam mused. His system hadn't settled since he'd set eyes on her.

"It's too late for that now. We're committed."

"Yeah." He let out a breath between his teeth and blocked Kirby from his mind. "Melanie Merrick Burgess is a close family friend and Harriet Merrick's daughter. She's a very elegant designer who doesn't seem to have any deep interest in painting. At a guess I'd say she'd be very supportive of the Fairchilds. Kirby recently broke off her engagement to Stuart Hiller."

"Interesting. When?"

"I don't have a date," Adam retorted. "And I didn't like pumping her about something that sensitive." He struggled with himself as McIntyre remained silent. "Sometime during the last couple months, I'd say, no longer. She's still smoldering." And hurting, he said to himself. He hadn't forgotten the look in her eyes. "I've been invited to a party this weekend. I should meet both Harriet Merrick and Hiller. In the meantime, I've had a break here. The place is riddled with secret passages."

"With what?"

"You heard me. With some luck, I'll have easy access throughout the house."

McIntyre grunted in approval. "You won't have any trouble recognizing it?"

"If he's got it, and if it's in the house, *and* if by some miracle I can find it in this anachronism, I'll recognize it." He switched off, and resisting the urge to throw the transmitter against the wall, dropped it back in the briefcase.

Clearing his mind, Adam rose and began to search the fireplace for the mechanism.

It took him nearly ten minutes, but he was rewarded with a groaning as a panel slid halfway open. He squeezed inside with a flashlight. It was both dank and musty, but he played the light against the wall until he found the inside switch. The panel squeaked closed and left him in the dark.

His footsteps echoed and he heard the skuddling sound of rodents. He ignored both. For a moment he stopped at the wall of Kirby's room. Telling himself he was only doing his job, he took the time to find the switch. But he wondered if she were already sleeping in the big four poster bed, under the wedding ring quilt.

He could press the button and join her. The hell with McIntyre and the job. The hell with everything but what lay beyond the wall. Procedure, he thought on an oath. He was sick to death of procedure. But Kirby had been right. Adam had a very firm grip on what was right and what was wrong.

He turned and continued down the passage.

Abruptly the corridor snaked off with steep stone steps forking to the left. Mounting them, he found himself in another corridor. A spider scrambled on the wall as he played his light over it. Kirby hadn't exaggerated much about the size. The third story, he decided, was as good a place to start as any.

He turned the first mechanism he found and slipped through the opening. Dust and dustcovers. Moving quietly, he began a slow, methodical search.

Kirby was restless. While Adam had been standing on the other side of the wall, fighting back the urge to open the panel, she'd been pacing her room. She'd considered going up to her studio. Work might calm her—but any work she did in this frame of mind would be trash. Frustrated, she sank down on the window seat. She could see the faint reflection of her own face and stared at it.

She wasn't completely in control. Almost any other flaw would've been easier to admit. Control was essential, and under the current circumstances, vital. The problem was getting it back.

The problem was, she corrected, Adam Haines.

Attraction? Yes, but that was simple and easily dealt with. There was something more twisted into it that was anything but simple. He could involve her, and once involved, nothing would be easily dealt with.

Laying her hands on the sill, she rested her head on them. He could hurt her. That was a first—a frightening first. Not a superficial blow to the pride or ego, Kirby admitted, but a hurt down deep where it counted; where it wouldn't heal.

Obviously, she told herself, forewarned was forearmed. She just wouldn't let him involve her, therefore she wouldn't let him hurt her. And that little piece of logic brought her right back to the control she didn't have. While she struggled to methodically untangle her thoughts, the beam of headlights distracted her.

Who'd be coming by at this time of night, she wondered without too much surprise. Fairchild had a habit of asking people over at odd hours. Kirby pressed her nose to the glass. A sound, not unlike Isabelle's growl, came from her throat.

"Of all the nerve," she muttered. "Of all the bloody nerve."

Springing up, she paced the floor three times before she grabbed a robe and left the room.

Above her head, Adam was about to re-enter the passageway when he, too, saw the beams. Automatically he switched off his flashlight and stepped beside the window. He watched the man step from a late model Mercedes and walk toward the house. Interesting, Adam decided. Abandoning the passageway, he slipped silently into the hall.

The sound of voices drifted up as he eased himself into the cover of a doorway and waited. Footsteps drew nearer. From his concealment, Adam watched Cards lead a slim, dark man up to Fairchild's tower studio.

"Mr. Hiller to see you, sir." Cards gave the information as if it were four in the afternoon rather than after midnight.

"Stuart, so nice of you to come." Fairchild's voice boomed through the doorway. "Come in, come in."

After counting to ten, Adam started to move toward the door Cards had shut when a flurry of white scrambled up the stairs. Swearing, he pressed back into the wall as Kirby passed, close enough to touch.

What the hell is this? he demanded, torn between frustration and the urge to laugh. Here he was, trapped in a doorway while people crept up tower steps in the middle of the night. While he watched, Kirby gathered the skirt of her robe around her knees and tip-toed up to the tower.

It was a nightmare, he decided. Women with floating hair sneaking around drafty corridors in filmy white. Secret passages. Clandestine meetings. A normal, sensible man wouldn't be involved in it for a minute. Then again, he'd stopped being completely sensible when he'd walked in the front door.

After Kirby reached the top landing, Adam moved closer. Her attention was focused on the studio door. Making a quick calculation, Adam moved up the steps behind her then melted into the shadows in the corner. With his eyes on her, he joined Kirby in the eavesdropping.

"What kind of fool do you think I am?" Stuart demanded. He stood beside Adam with only the wall separating them.

"Whatever kind you prefer. Makes no difference to me. Have a seat, my boy."

"Listen to me, we had a deal. How long did you think it would take before I found out you'd double-crossed me?"

"Actually I didn't think it would take you quite so long." Smiling, Fairchild rubbed a thumb over his clay hawk. "Not as clever as I thought you were, Stuart. You should've discovered the switch weeks ago. Not that it wasn't superb," he added with a touch of pride. "But a smart man would've had the painting authenticated."

Because the conversation confused her, Kirby pressed even closer to the door. She tucked her hair behind her ear as if to hear more clearly. Untended, her robe fell open, revealing a thin excuse for a nightgown and a great deal of smooth golden skin. In his corner, Adam shifted and swore to himself.

"We had a deal—" Stuart's voice rose, but Fairchild cut him off with no more than a wave of his hand.

"Don't tell me you believe in that nonsense about honor among thieves? Time to grow up if you want to play in the big leagues."

"I want the Rembrandt, Fairchild."

Kirby stiffened. Because his attention was now fully focused on the battle in the tower, Adam didn't notice. By God, he thought grimly, the old bastard did have it.

"Sue me," Fairchild invited. Kirby could hear the shrug in his voice.

"Hand it over, or I'll break your scrawny neck."

For a full ten seconds, Fairchild watched calmly as Stuart's face turned a deep, dull red. "You won't get it that way. And I should warn you that threats make me irritable. You see…" Slowly he picked up a rag and began to wipe some excess clay from his hands. "I didn't care for your treatment of Kirby. No, I didn't care for it at all."

Abruptly he was no longer the harmless eccentric. He was neither cherub nor gnome, but a man. A dangerous one. "I knew she'd never go as far as marrying you. She's far too bright. But your threats, once she told you off, annoyed me. When I'm annoyed, I tend to be vindictive. A flaw," he said amiably. "But that's just the way I'm made." The pale eyes were cold and calm on Stuart's. "I'm still annoyed, Stuart. I'll let you know when I'm ready to deal. In the meantime, stay away from Kirby."

"You're not going to get away with this."

"I hold all the cards." In an impatient gesture, he brushed Stuart aside. "I have the Rembrandt, and only I know where it is. If you become a nuisance, which you're dangerously close to becoming, I may decide to keep it. Unlike you, I have no pressing need for money." He smiled, but the chill remained in his eyes. "One should never live above one's means, Stuart. That's my advice."

Impotent, intimidated, Stuart loomed over the little man at the work table. He was strong enough, and furious enough, to have snapped Fairchild's neck with his hands. But he wouldn't have the Rembrandt, or the money he so desperately needed. "Before we're done, you'll pay," Stuart promised. "I won't be made a fool of."

"Too late," Fairchild told him easily. "Run along now. You can find your way out without disturbing Cards, can't you?"

As if he were already alone, Fairchild went back to his hawk.

Swiftly, Kirby looked around for a hiding place. For one ridiculous moment, Adam thought she'd try to ease herself into the corner he occupied. The moment she started to cross the hall toward him, the handle of the door turned. She'd left her move too late. With her back pressed against the wall, Kirby closed her eyes and pretended to be invisible.

Stuart wrenched open the door and stalked from the room, blind with rage. Without a backward glance he plunged down the steps. His face, Adam noted as he passed, was murderous. At the moment, he lacked a weapon. But if he found one, he wouldn't hesitate.

Kirby stood, still and silent as the footsteps receded. She sucked in a deep breath, then let it out on a huff. What now? *What now?* she thought and wanted to just bury her face in her hands and surrender. Instead she straightened her shoulders and went in to confront her father.

"Papa." The word was quiet and accusing. Fairchild's head jerked up, but his surprise was quickly masked by a genial smile.

"Hello, love. My hawk's beginning to breathe. Come have a look."

She took another deep breath. All of her life she'd loved him, stood by him. Adored him. None of that had ever stopped her from being angry with him. Slowly, keeping her eyes on him, she crossed the front panels of her robe and tied the sash. As she approached, Fairchild thought she looked like a gunslinger buckling on his six gun. She wouldn't, he thought with a surge of pride, intimidate like Hiller.

"Apparently you haven't kept me up to date," she began. "A riddle, Papa. What do Philip Fairchild, Stuart Hiller and Rembrandt have in common?"

"You've always been clever at riddles, my sweet."

"*Now,* Papa."

"Just business." He gave her a quick, hearty smile as he wondered just how much he'd have to tell her.

"Let's be specific, shall we?" She moved so that only the table separated them. "And don't give me that blank, foolish look. It won't work." Bending over, she stared directly into his eyes. "I heard quite a bit while I was outside. Tell me the rest."

"Eavesdropping." He made a disapproving tsk-tsk. "Rude."

"I come by it honestly. Now tell me or I'll annihilate your hawk." Sweeping up her arm, she held her palm three inches above his clay.

"Vicious brat." With his bony fingers, he grabbed her wrist, each knowing who'd win if it came down to it. He gave a windy sigh. "All right."

With a nod, Kirby removed her hand then folded her arms under her breasts. The habitual gesture had him sighing again.

"Stuart came to me with a little proposition some time ago. You know, of course, he hasn't a cent to his name, no matter what he pretends."

"Yes, I know he wanted to marry me for my money." No one but her father would've detected the slight tightening in her voice.

"I didn't bring that up to hurt you." His hand reached for hers in the bond that had been formed when she'd taken her first breath.

"I know, Papa." She squeezed his hand then stuck both of hers in the pockets of her robe. "My pride suffered. It has to happen now and again, I suppose. But I don't care for humility," she said with sudden fierceness. "I don't care for it one bloody bit." With a toss of her head, she looked down at him. "The rest."

"Well." Fairchild puffed out his cheeks then blew out the breath. "Among his other faults, Stuart's greedy. He needed a large sum of money, and didn't see why he had to work for it. He decided to help himself to the Rembrandt self-portrait from Harriet's gallery."

"He *stole* it?" Kirby's eyes grew huge. "Great buckets of bedbugs! I wouldn't have given him credit for that much nerve."

"He thought himself clever." Rising, Fairchild walked to the little sink in the corner to wash off his hands. "Harriet was going on her safari, and there'd be no one to question the disappearance for several weeks. Stuart's a bit dictatorial with the staff at the gallery."

"It's such a treat to flog underlings."

"In any case—" lovingly, Fairchild draped his hawk for the night "—he came to me with an offer—a rather paltry offer, too—if I'd do the forgery for the Rembrandt's replacement."

She hadn't thought he could do anything to surprise her. Certainly nothing to hurt her. "Papa, it's Harriet's Rembrandt," she said in shock.

"Now, Kirby, you know I'm fond of Harriet. Very fond." He put a comforting arm around her shoulders. "Our Stuart has a very small brain. He handed over the Rembrandt when I said I needed it to do the copy." Fairchild shook his head. "There wasn't any challenge to it, Kirby. Hardly any fun at all."

"Pity," she said dryly and dropped into a chair.

"Then I told him I didn't need the original any longer, and gave him the copy instead. He never suspected." Fairchild linked his hands behind his back and stared up at the ceiling. "I wish you'd seen it. It was superlative. It was one of Rembrandt's later works, you know. Rough textures, such luminous depth—"

"Papa!" Kirby interrupted what would've become a lecture.

"Oh, yes, yes." With an effort, Fairchild controlled himself. "I told him it'd take just a little more time to complete the copy and treat it for the illusion of age. He bought it. Gullibility," Fairchild added and clucked his tongue. "It's been almost three weeks, and he just got around to having the painting tested. I made certain it wouldn't stand up to the most basic of tests, of course."

"Of course," Kirby murmured.

"Now he has to leave the copy in the gallery. And I have the original."

She gave herself a moment to absorb all he'd told her. It didn't make any difference in how she felt. Furious. "Why, Papa? Why did you do this! It isn't like all the others. It's Harriet."

"Now, Kirby, don't lose control. You've such a nasty temper." He did his best to look small and helpless. "I'm much too old to cope with it. Remember my blood pressure."

"Blood pressure be hanged." She glared up at him with fury surging into her eyes. "Don't think you're going to get around me with that. Old?" she tossed back. "You're still your youngest child."

"I feel a spell coming on," he said, inspired by Kirby's own warning two days before. He pressed a trembling hand to his heart and staggered. "I'll end up a useless heap of cold spaghetti. Ah, the paintings I might have done. The world's losing a genius."

Clenching her fists, Kirby beat them on his work table. Tools bounced and clattered while she let out a long wail. Protective, Fairchild placed his hands around his hawk and waited for the crisis to pass. At length, she slumped back in the chair, breathless.

"You used to do better than that," he observed. "I think you're mellowing."

"Papa." Kirby clamped her teeth to keep from grinding them. "I know I'll be forced to beat you about the head and ears, then I'll be arrested for patricide. You know I've a terror of closed-in places. I'd go mad in prison. Do you want that on your conscience?"

"Kirby, have I ever given you cause for one moment's worry?"

"Don't force me into a recital, Papa, it's after midnight. What have you done with the Rembrandt?"

"Done with it?" He frowned and fiddled with the cover of his hawk. "What do you mean, done with it?"

"Where is it?" she asked, carefully spacing the words. "You can't leave a painting like that lying around the house, particularly when you've chosen to have company."

"Company? Oh, you mean, Adam. Fine boy. I'm fond of him already." His eyebrows wiggled twice. "You seem to be finding him agreeable."

Kirby narrowed her eyes. "Leave Adam out of this."

"Dear, dear, dear." Fairchild grinned lavishly. "And I thought you'd brought him up."

"Where *is* the Rembrandt?" All claim to patience disintegrated. Briefly, she considered banging her head on the table, but she'd given up that particular ploy at ten.

"Safe and secure, my sweet." Fairchild's voice was calm and pleased. "Safe and secure."

"Here? In the house?"

"Of course." He gave her an astonished look. "You don't think I'd keep it anywhere else?"

"Where?"

"You don't need to know everything." With a flourish he whipped off his painting smock and tossed it over a chair. "Just content yourself that it's safe, hidden with appropriate respect and affection."

"Papa."

"Kirby." He smiled—a gentle father's smile. "A child must trust her parent, must abide by the wisdom of his years. You do trust me, don't you?"

"Yes, of course, but—"

He cut her off with the first bars of "Daddy's Little Girl" in a wavering falsetto.

Kirby moaned and lowered her head to the table. When would she learn? And how was she going to deal with him this time? He continued to sing until the giggles welled up and escaped. "You're incorrigible." She lifted her head and took a deep breath. "I have this terrible feeling that you're leaving out a mountain of details and that I'm going to go along with you anyway."

"Details, Kirby." His hand swept them aside. "The world's too full of details, they clutter things up. Remember, art reflects life, and life's an illusion. Come now, I'm tired." He walked to her and held out his hand. "Walk your old Papa to bed."

Defeated, she accepted his hand and stood. Never, never would she learn. And always, always would she adore him. Together they walked from the room.

Adam watched as they started down the steps, arm in arm.

"Papa..." Only feet away from Adam's hiding place, Kirby stopped. "There is, of course, a logical reason for all this?"

"Kirby." Adam could see the mobile face move into calm, sober lines. "Have I ever done anything without a sensible, logical reason?"

She started with a near soundless chuckle. In moments her laughter rang out, rich and musical. It echoed back, faint and ghostly until she rested her head against her father's shoulder. In the half light, with her eyes shining, Adam thought she'd never looked more alluring. "Oh my Papa," she began in a clear contralto. "To me he is so wonderful." Linking her arm through Fairchild's, she continued down the steps.

Rather pleased with himself, and with his offspring, Fairchild joined her in his wavery falsetto. Their mixed voices drifted over Adam until the distance swallowed them.

Leaving the shadows, he stood at the head of the stairway. Once he heard Kirby's laugh, then there was silence.

"Curiouser and curiouser," he murmured.

Both Fairchilds were probably mad. They fascinated him.

Chapter 5

In the morning the sky was gray and the rain sluggish. Adam was tempted to roll over, close his eyes and pretend he was in his own well-organized home where a housekeeper tended to the basics and there wasn't a gargoyle in sight. Partly from curiosity, partly from courage, he rose and prepared to deal with the day.

From what he'd overheard the night before, he didn't count on learning much from Kirby. Apparently she'd known less about the matter of the Rembrandt than he. Adam was equally sure that no matter how much he prodded and poked, Fairchild would let nothing slip. He might look innocent and harmless, but he was as shrewd as they came. And potentially dangerous, Adam mused, remembering how cleanly Fairchild had dealt with Hiller.

The best course of action remained the nightly searches with the aid of the passages. The days he determined for his own sanity to spend painting.

I shouldn't be here in the first place, Adam told himself as he stood in the shower under a strong cold spray of water. If it hadn't been for the fact that Mac tantalized me with the Rembrandt, I *wouldn't* be here. The last time, he promised himself as he toweled off. The very last time.

Once the Fairchild hassle was over, painting would not only be his first order of business, it would be his only business.

Dressed, and content with the idea of ending his secondary career in a few more weeks, Adam walked down the hallway thinking of coffee. Kirby's door was wide open. As he passed, he glanced in. Frowning, he stopped, walked back and stood in the doorway.

"Good morning, Adam. Isn't it a lovely day?" She smiled, upside down, as she stood on her head in the corner.

Deliberately he glanced at the window to make sure he was on solid ground. "It's raining."

"Don't you like the rain? I do." She rubbed her nose with the back of her hand. "Look at it this way, there must be dozens of places where the sun's shining. It's all relative. Did you sleep well?"

"Yes." Even in her current position, Adam could see that her face glowed, showing no signs of a restless night.

"Come in and wait a minute, I'll go down to breakfast with you."

He walked over to stand directly in front of her. "Why are you standing on your head?"

"It's a theory of mine." She crossed her ankles against the wall while her hair pooled onto the carpet. "Could you sit down a minute? It's hard for me to talk to you when your head's up there and mine's down here."

Knowing he'd regret it, Adam crouched. Her sweater had slipped up, showing a thin line of smooth midriff.

"Thanks. My theory is that all night I've been horizontal, and most of the day I'll be right side up. So..." Somehow she managed to shrug. "I stand on my head in the morning and before bed. That way the blood can slosh around a bit."

Adam rubbed his nose between his thumb and forefinger. "I think I understand. That terrifies me."

"You should try it."

"I'll just let my blood stagnate, thanks."

"Suit yourself. You'd better stand back, I'm coming up."

She dropped her feet and righted herself with a quick athletic agility that surprised him. Facing him, she pushed at the hair that floated into her eyes. As she tossed it back she gave him a long, slow smile.

"Your face is red," he murmured, more in his own defense than for any other reason.

"Can't be helped, it's part of the process." She'd spent a good many hours arguing with herself the night before. This morning she'd decided to let things happen as they happened. "It's the only time I blush," she told him. "So, if you'd like to say something embarrassing... or flattering...?"

Against his better judgment he touched her, circling her waist with his hands. She didn't move back, didn't move forward, but simply waited. "Your blush is already fading so it seems I've missed my chance."

"You can give it another try tomorrow. Hungry?"

"Yes." Her lips made him hungry, but he wasn't ready to test himself quite yet. "I want to go through your clothes after breakfast."

"Oh, really?" She drew out the word, catching her tongue between her teeth.

His brow lifted, but only she was aware of the gesture. "For the painting."

"You don't want to do a nude." The humor in her eyes faded into boredom as she drew away. "That's the usual line."

"I don't waste my time with lines." He studied her—the cool gray eyes that could warm with laughter, the haughty mouth that could invite and promise with no more than a smile. "I'm going to paint you because you were meant to be painted. I'm going to make love with you for exactly the same reason."

Her expression didn't change, but her pulse rate did. Kirby wasn't foolish enough to pretend even to herself it was anger. Anger and excitement were two different things. "How decisive and arrogant of you," she drawled. Strolling over to her dresser, she picked up her brush and ran it quickly through her hair. "I haven't agreed to pose for you, Adam, nor have I agreed to sleep with you." She flicked the brush through a last time then set it down. "In fact, I've serious doubts that I'll do either. Shall we go?"

Before she could get to the door, he had her. The speed surprised her, if the strength didn't. She'd hoped to annoy him, but when she tossed her head back to look at him, she didn't see temper. She saw cool, patient determination. Nothing could have been more unnerving.

Then he had her close so that his face was a blur and his mouth was dominant. She didn't resist. Kirby rarely resisted what she wanted. Instead she let the heat wind through her in a slow continuous stream that was somehow both terrifying and peaceful.

Desire. Wasn't that how she'd always imagined it would be with the right man? Wasn't that what she'd been waiting for since the first moment she'd discovered herself a woman? It was here now. Kirby opened her arms to it.

His heartbeat wasn't steady and it should have been. His mind wasn't clear and it had to be. How could he win with her when he lost ground every time he was around her? If he followed through on his promise—or threat—that they'd be lovers, how much more would he lose? And gain, he thought as he let himself become steeped in her. The risk was worth taking.

"You'll pose for me," he said against her mouth. "And you'll make love with me. There's no choice."

That was the word that stopped her. That was the phrase that forced her to resist. She'd always have a choice. "I don't—"

"For either of us," Adam finished as he released her. "We'll decide on the clothes after breakfast." Because he didn't want to give either of them a chance to speak, he propelled her from the room.

An hour later, he propelled her back.

She'd been serene during the meal. But he hadn't been fooled. Livid was what she was and livid was exactly how he wanted her. She didn't like to be outmaneuvered, even on a small point. It gave him a surge of satisfaction to be able to do so. The defiant, sulky look in her eyes was exactly what he wanted for the portrait.

"Red, I think," he stated. "It would suit you best."

Kirby waved a hand at her closet and flopped backward onto her bed. Staring up at the ceiling, she thought through her position. It was true she'd always refused to be painted, except by her father. She hadn't wanted anyone else to get that close to her. As an artist, she knew just how intimate the relationship was between painter and subject, be the subject a person or a bowl of fruit. She'd never been willing to share herself with anyone to that extent.

But Adam was different. She could, if she chose, tell herself it was because of his talent, and because he wanted to paint her, not flatter her. It wasn't a lie, but it wasn't quite the truth. Still, Kirby was comfortable with partial truths in certain cases. If she were honest, she had to admit that she was curious to see just how she'd look from his perspective, and yet she wasn't entirely comfortable with that.

Moving only her eyes, she watched him as he rummaged through her closet.

He didn't have to know what was going on in her head. Certainly she was skilled in keeping her thoughts to herself. It might be a challenge to do so under the sharp eyes of an artist. It might be interesting to see just how difficult she could make it for him. She folded her hands demurely on her stomach.

While Kirby was busy with her self-debate, Adam looked through an incredible variety of clothes. Some were perfect for an orphan, others for an eccentric teenager. He wondered if she'd actually worn the purple mini skirt and just how she'd looked in it. Elegant gowns from Paris and New York hung haphazardly with army surplus. If clothes reflected the person, there was more than one Kirby Fairchild. He wondered just how many she'd show him.

He discarded one outfit after another. This one was too drab, that one too chic. He found a pair of baggy overalls thrown over the same hanger with a slinky sequin dress with a two-thousand dollar label. Pushing aside a three-piece suit perfect for an assistant D.A., he found it.

Scarlet silk. It was undoubtedly expensive, but not chic in the way he imagined Melanie Burgess would design. The square-necked bodice tapered to a narrow waist before the material flared into a full skirt. There were flounces at the hem and underskirts of white and black and fuchsia. The sleeves were short and puffed, running with stripes of the same colors. It was made for a wealthy gypsy. It was perfect.

"This." Adam carried it to the bed and stood over Kirby. With a frown, she continued to stare up at the ceiling. "Put it on and come up to the studio. I'll do some sketches."

She spoke without looking at him. "Do you realize that not once have you asked me to pose for you? You told me you wanted to paint me, you told me you were going to paint me, but you've never *asked* if you could paint me." With her hands still folded, one finger began to tap. "Instinct tells me you're basically a gentleman, Adam. Perhaps you've just forgotten to say please."

"I haven't forgotten." He tossed the dress across the bottom of the bed. "But I think you hear far too many pleases from men. You're a woman who brings men to their knees with the bat of the eye. I'm not partial to kneeling.'' No, he wasn't partial to kneeling, and it was becoming imperative that he handle the controls, for both of them. Bending over, he put his hands on either side of her head then sat beside her. "And I'm just as used to getting my own way as you are."

She studied him, thinking over his words and her position. "Then again, I haven't batted my eyes at you yet."

"Haven't you?" he murmured.

He could smell her, that wild, untamed fragrance that was suited to isolated winter nights. Her lips pouted, not by design, but mood. It was that that tempted him. He had to taste them. He did so lightly, as he'd intended. Just a touch, just a taste, then he'd go about his business. But her mouth yielded to him as the whole woman hadn't. Or perhaps it conquered.

Desire scorched him. Fire was all he could relate to. Flames and heat and smoke. That was her taste. Smoke and temptation and a promise of unreasonable delights.

He tasted, but it was no longer enough. He had to touch.

Her body was small, delicate, something a man might fear to take. He did, but no longer for her sake. For his own. Small and delicate, she might be, but she could slice a man in two. Of that he was certain. But as he touched, as he tasted, he didn't give a damn.

Never had he wanted a woman more. She made him feel like a teenager in the back seat of a car, like a man paying for the best whore in a French bordello, like a husband nuzzling into the security of a wife. Her complexities were more erotic than satin and lace and smoky light—the soft, agile mouth, the strong, determined hands. He wasn't certain he'd ever escape from either. In possessing her, he'd invite an endless cycle of complications, of struggles, of excitement. She was an opiate. She was a dive from a cliff. If he wasn't careful, he was going to overdose and hit the rocks.

It cost him more than he would have believed to draw back. She lay with her eyes half closed, her mouth just parted. Don't get involved, he told himself frantically. Get the Rembrandt and walk away. That's what you came to do.

"Adam..." She whispered his name as if she'd never said it before. It felt so beautiful on her tongue. The only thought that stayed with her was that no one had ever made her feel like this. No one else ever would. Something was opening inside her, but she wouldn't fight it. She'd give. The innocence in her eyes was real, emotional not physical. Seeing it, Adam felt desire flare again.

She's a witch, he told himself. Circe. Lorelei. He had to pull back before he forgot that. "You'll have to change."

"Adam..." Still swimming, she reached up and touched his face.

"Emphasize your eyes." He stood before he could take the dive.

"My eyes?" Mind blank, body throbbing, she stared up at him.

"And leave your hair loose." He strode to the door as she struggled up to her elbows. "Twenty minutes."

She wouldn't let him see the hurt. She wouldn't allow herself to feel the rejection. "You're a cool one, aren't you?" she said softly. "And as smooth as any I've ever run across. You might find yourself on your knees yet."

She was right—he could've strangled her for it. "That's a risk I'll have to take." With a nod, he walked through the door. "Twenty minutes," he called back.

Kirby clenched her fists together then slowly relaxed them. "On your knees," she promised herself. "I swear it."

Alone in Kirby's studio, Adam searched for the mechanism to the passageway. He looked mainly from curiosity. It was doubtful he'd need to rummage through a room that he'd been given free run in, but he was satisfied when he located the control. The panel creaked open, as noisily as all the others he'd found. After a quick look inside, he shut it again and went back to the first order of business—painting.

It was never a job, but it wasn't always a pleasure. The need to paint was a demand that could be soft and gentle, or sharp and cutting. Not a job, but work certainly, sometimes every bit as exhausting as digging a trench with a pick and shovel.

Adam was a meticulous artist as he was a meticulous man. Conventional, as Kirby had termed him, perhaps. But he wasn't rigid. He was as orderly as she wasn't, but his creative process was remarkably similar to hers. She might stare at a piece of wood for an hour until she saw the life in it. He would do the same with a canvas. She would feel a jolt, a physical release the moment she saw what she'd been searching for. He'd feel that same jolt when something would leap out at him from one of his dozens of sketches.

Now he was only preparing, and he was as calm and ordered as his equipment. On an easel he set the canvas, blank and waiting. Carefully, he selected three pieces of charcoal. He'd begin with them. He was going over his first informal sketches when he heard her footsteps.

She paused in the doorway, tossed her head and stared at him. With deliberate care, he set his pad back on the work table.

Her hair fell loose and rich over the striped silk shoulders. At a movement, the gold hoops at her ears and the half dozen gold bracelets on her arm jangled. Her eyes, darkened and sooty, still smoldered with temper. Without effort he could picture her whirling around an open fire to the sound of violins and tambourines.

Aware of the image she projected, Kirby put both hands on her hips and walked into the room. The full scarlet skirt flowed around her legs. Standing in front of him, she whirled around twice, turning her head each time so that she watched him over her shoulder. The scent of wood smoke and roses flowed into the room.

"You want to paint Katrina's picture, eh?" Her voice lowered into a sultry Slavic accent as she ran a fingertip down his cheek. Insolence, challenge, and then a laugh that skidded warm and dangerous over his skin. "First you cross her palm with silver."

He'd have given her anything. What man wouldn't? Fighting her, fighting himself, he pulled out a cigarette. "Over by the east window," he said easily. "The light's better there."

No, he wouldn't get off so easy. Behind the challenge and the insolence, her body still trembled for him. She wouldn't let him know it.. "How much you pay?" she demanded, swirling away in a flurry of scarlet and silk. "Katrina not come free."

"Scale." He barely resisted the urge to grab her by the hair and drag her back. "And you won't get a dime until I'm finished."

In an abrupt change Kirby brushed and smoothed her skirts. "Is something wrong?" she asked mildly. "Perhaps you don't like the dress after all."

He crushed out his cigarette in one grinding motion. "Let's get started."

"I thought we already had," she murmured. Her eyes were luminous and amused. He wanted to choke her every bit as much as he wanted to crawl for her. "You insisted on painting."

"Don't push me too far, Kirby. You have a tendency to bring out my baser side."

"I don't think I can be blamed for that. Maybe you've locked it up too long." Because she'd gotten precisely the reaction she'd wanted, she became completely cooperative. "Now, where do you want me to stand?"

"By the east window."

Tie score, she thought with satisfaction as she obliged him.

He spoke only when he had to—tilt your chin higher, turn your head. Within moments he was able to turn the anger and the desire into concentration. The rain fell, but its sound was muffled against the thick glass windows. With the tower door nearly closed, there wasn't another sound.

He watched her, studied her, absorbed her, but the man and the artist were working together. Perhaps by putting her on canvas, he'd understand her...and himself. Adam swept the charcoal over the canvas and began.

Now she could watch him, knowing that he was turned inward. She'd seen dozens of artists work; the old, the young, the talented, the amateur. Adam was, as she'd suspected, different.

He wore a sweater, one he was obviously at home in, but no smock. Even as he sketched he stood straight, as though his nature demanded that he remain always alert. That was one of the things she'd noticed about him first. He was always watching. A true artist did, she knew, but there seemed to be something more.

She called him conventional, knowing it wasn't quite true. Not quite. What was it about him that didn't fit into the mold he'd been fashioned for? Tall, lean, attractive, aristocratic, wealthy, successful, and...daring? That was the word that came to mind though she wasn't completely sure why.

There was something reckless about him that appealed to her. It balanced the maturity, the dependability she hadn't known she'd wanted in a man. He'd be a rock to hold on to during an earthquake. And he'd be the earthquake. She was, Kirby realized, sinking fast. The trick would be to keep him from realizing it and making a fool of herself. Still, beneath it all, she liked him. That simple.

Adam glanced up to see her smiling at him. It was disarming, sweet and uncomplicated. Something

warned him that Kirby without guards was far more
dangerous than Kirby with them. When she let hers
drop, he put his in place.

"Doesn't Hiller paint a bit?"

He saw her smile fade and tried not to regret it. "A
bit."

"Haven't you posed for him?"

"No."

"Why not?"

The ice that came into her eyes wasn't what he
wanted for the painting. The man and artist warred as
he continued to sketch. "Let's say I didn't care much
for his work."

"I suppose I can take that as a compliment to
mine."

She gave him a long, neutral look. "If you like."

Deceit was part of the job, he reminded himself.
What he'd heard in Fairchild's studio left him no
choice. "I'm surprised he didn't make an issue of it,
being in love with you."

"He wasn't." She bit off the words and ice turned
to heat.

"He asked you to marry him."

"One hasn't anything to do with the other."

He looked up and saw she said exactly what she
meant. "Doesn't it?"

"I agreed to marry him without loving him."

He held the charcoal an inch from the canvas, forgetting the painting. "Why?"

While she stared at him he saw the anger fade. For
a moment she was simply a woman at her most vulnerable. "Timing," she murmured. "It's probably the
most important factor governing our lives. If it hadn't

been for timing, Romeo and Juliet would've raised a half dozen children."

He was beginning to understand, and understanding only made him more uncomfortable. "You thought it was time to get married?"

"Stuart's attractive, very polished, charming, and I'd thought harmless. I realized the last thing I wanted was a polished, charming, harmless husband. Still, I thought he loved me. I didn't break the engagement for a long time because I thought he'd make a convenient husband, and one who wouldn't demand too much." It sounded empty. It had been empty. "One who'd give me children."

"You want children?"

The anger was back, quickly. "Is there something wrong with that?" she demanded. "Do you think it strange that I'd want a family?" She made a quick, furious movement that had the gold jangling again. "This might come as a shock, but I have needs and feelings almost like a real person. And I don't have to justify myself to you."

She was halfway to the door before he could stop her. "Kirby, I'm sorry." When she tried to jerk out of his hold, he tightened it. "I *am* sorry."

"For what?" she tossed back.

"For hurting you," he murmured. "With stupidity."

Her shoulders relaxed under his hands, slowly, so that he knew it cost her. Guilt flared again. "All right. You hit a nerve, that's all." Deliberately she removed his hands from her shoulders and stepped back. He'd rather she'd slapped him. "Give me a cigarette, will you?"

She took one from him and let him light it before she turned away again. "When I accepted Stuart's proposal—"

"You don't have to tell me anything."

"I don't leave things half done." Some of the insolence was back when she whirled back to him. For some reason it eased Adam's guilt. "When I accepted, I told Stuart I wasn't in love with him. It didn't seem fair otherwise. If two people are going to have a relationship that means anything, it has to start out honestly, don't you think?"

He thought of the transmitter tucked into his briefcase. He thought of McIntyre waiting for the next report. "Yes."

She nodded. It was one area where she wasn't flexible. "I told him that what I wanted from him was fidelity and children, and in return I'd give him those things and as much affection as I could." She toyed with the cigarette, taking one of her quick nervous drags. "When I realized things just wouldn't work for either of us that way, I went to see him. I didn't do it carelessly, casually. It was very difficult for me. Can you understand that?"

"Yes, I understand that."

It helped, she realized. More than Melanie's sympathy, more even than her father's unspoken support, Adam's simple understanding helped. "It didn't go well. I'd known there'd be an argument, but I hadn't counted on it getting so out of hand. He made a few choice remarks on my maternal abilities and my track record. Anyway, with all the blood and bone being strewn about, the real reason for him wanting to marry me came out."

She took a last puff on the cigarette and crushed it out before she dropped into a chair. "He never loved me. He'd been unfaithful all along. I don't suppose it mattered." But she fell silent, knowing it did. "All the time he was pretending to care for me, he was using me." When she looked up again, the hurt was back in her eyes. She didn't know it—she'd have hated it. "Can you imagine how it feels to find out that all the time someone was holding you, talking with you, he was thinking of how you could be useful?" She picked up the piece of half-formed wood that would be her anger. "Useful," she repeated. "What a nasty word. I haven't bounced back from it as well as I should have."

He forgot McIntyre, the Rembrandt and the job he still had to do. Walking over, he sat beside her and closed his hand over hers. Under them was her anger. "I can't imagine any man thinking of you as useful."

When she looked up, her smile was already spreading. "What a nice thing to say. The perfect thing." Too perfect for her rapidly crumbling defenses. Because she knew it would take so little to have her turning to him now and later, she lightened the mood. "I'm glad you're going to be there Saturday."

"At the party?"

"You can send me long, smoldering looks and everyone'll think I jilted Stuart for you. I'm fond of petty revenge."

He laughed and brought her hands to his lips. "Don't change," he told her with a sudden intenseness that had her uncertain again.

"I don't plan on it. Adam, I—Oh, chicken fat, what're you doing here? This is a private conversation."

Wary, Adam turned his head and watched Montique bounce into the room. "He won't spread gossip."

"That isn't the point. I've told you you're not allowed in here."

Ignoring her, Montique scurried over and with an awkward leap plopped into Adam's lap. "Cute little devil," Adam decided as he scratched the floppy ears.

"Ah, Adam, I wouldn't do that."

"Why?"

"You're only asking for trouble."

"Don't be absurd. He's harmless."

"Oh, yes, he is. *She* isn't." Kirby nodded her head toward the doorway as Isabelle slinked through. "Now you're in for it. I warned you." Tossing back her head, Kirby met Isabelle's cool look equally. "I had nothing to do with it."

Isabelle blinked twice then shifted her gaze to Adam. Deciding her responsibility had ended, Kirby sighed and rose. "There's nothing I can do," she told Adam and patted his shoulder. "You asked for it." With this, she swept out of the room, giving the cat a wide berth.

"I didn't ask him to come up here," Adam began, scowling down at Isabelle. "And there can't be any harm in—Oh, God," he murmured. "She's got me doing it."

Chapter 6

Let's walk," Kirby demanded when the afternoon grew late and Fairchild had yet to budge from his studio. Nor would he budge, she knew, until the Van Gogh was completed down to the smallest detail. If she didn't get out and forget about her father's pet project for awhile, she knew she'd go mad.

"It's raining," Adam pointed out as he lingered over coffee.

"You mentioned that before." Kirby pushed away her own coffee and rose. "All right then, I'll have Cards bring you a lap robe and a nice cup of tea."

"Is that a psychological attack?"

"Did it work?"

"I'll get a jacket." He strode from the room, ignoring her quiet chuckle.

When they walked outside, the fine misting rain fell over them. Leaves streamed with it. Thin fingers of fog twisted along the ground. Adam hunched inside his jacket thinking it was miserable weather for a walk. Kirby strolled along with her face lifted to the sky.

He'd planned to spend the afternoon on the painting, but perhaps this was better. If he was going to capture her with colors and brush strokes, he should get to know her better. No easy task, Adam mused, but a strangely appealing one.

The air was heavy with the fragrance of fall, the sky gloomy. For the first time since he'd met her, Adam sensed a serenity in Kirby. They walked in silence, with the rain flowing over them.

She was content. It was an odd feeling for her to identify as she felt it so rarely. With her hand in his, she was content to walk along as the fog moved along the ground and the chilly drizzle fell over them. She was glad of the rain, of the chill and the gloom. Later, there would be time for a roaring fire and warm brandy.

"Adam, do you see the bed of mums over there?"

"Hmm?"

"The mums, I want to pick some. You'll have to be the lookout."

"Lookout for what?" He shook wet hair out of his eyes.

"For Jamie, of course. He doesn't like anyone messing with his flowers."

"They're your flowers."

"No, they're Jamie's."

"He works for you."

"What does that have to do with it?" She put a hand on his shoulder as she scanned the area. "If he catches me, he'll get mad, then he won't save me any leaves. I'll be quick—I've done this before."

"But if you—"

"There's no time to argue. Now, you watch that window there. He's probably in the kitchen having coffee with Tulip. Give me a signal when you see him."

Whether he went along with her because it was simpler, or because he was getting into the spirit of things despite himself, Adam wasn't sure. But he walked over to the window and peeked inside. Jamie sat at a huge round table with a mug of coffee in both frail hands. Turning, he nodded a go-ahead to Kirby.

She moved like lightning, dashing to the flower bed and plucking at stems. Dark and wet, her hair fell forward to curtain her face as she loaded her arms with autumn flowers. She should be painted like this, as well, Adam mused. In the fog, with her arms full of wet flowers. Perhaps it would be possible to capture those odd little snatches of innocence in the portrait.

Idly he glanced back in the window. With a ridiculous jolt of panic, he saw Jamie rise and head for the kitchen door. Forgetting logic, Adam dashed toward her.

"He's coming."

Surprisingly swift, Kirby leaped over the bed of flowers and kept on going. Even though he was running full stride, Adam didn't catch her until they'd rounded the side of the house. Giggling and out of breath, she collapsed against him.

"We made it!"

"Just," he agreed. His own heart was thudding—from the race? Maybe. He was breathless—from the game? Perhaps. But they were wet and close and the fog was rising. It didn't seem he had a choice any longer.

With his eyes on hers, he brushed the dripping hair back from her face. Her cheeks were cool, wet and smooth. Yet her mouth, when his lowered to it, was warm and waiting.

She hadn't planned it this way. If she'd had the time to think, she'd have said she didn't want it this way. She didn't want to be weak. She didn't want her mind muddled. It didn't seem she had a choice any longer.

He could taste the rain on her, fresh and innocent. He could smell the sharp tang of the flowers that were crushed between them. He couldn't keep his hands out of her hair, the soft, heavy tangle of it. He wanted her closer. He wanted all of her, not in the way he'd first wanted her, but in every way. The need was no longer the simple need of a man for woman, but of him for her. Exclusive, imperative, impossible.

She'd wanted to fall in love, but she'd wanted to plan it out in her own way, in her own time. It wasn't supposed to happen in a crash and a roar that left her trembling. It wasn't supposed to happen without her permission. Shaken, Kirby drew back. It wasn't going to happen until she was ready. That was that. Nerves taut again, she made herself smile.

"It looks like we've done a good job of squashing them." When he would've drawn her back, Kirby thrust the flowers at him. "They're for you."

"For me?" Adam looked down at the mums they held between them.

"Yes, don't you like flowers?"

"I like flowers," he murmured. However unintentionally, she'd moved him as much with the gift as with the kiss. "I don't think anyone's given me flowers before."

"No?" She gave him a long, considering look. She'd been given floods of them over the years, orchids, lilies, roses and more roses until they'd meant little more than nothing. Her smile came slowly as she touched a hand to his chest. "I'd've picked more if I'd known."

Behind them a window was thrown open. "Don't you know better than to stand in the rain and neck?" Fairchild demanded. "If you want to nuzzle, come inside. I can't stand sneezing and sniffling!" The window shut with a bang.

"You're terribly wet," Kirby commented as if she hadn't noticed the steadily falling rain. She linked her arm with his and walked to the door that was opened by the ever efficient Cards.

"Thank you." Kirby peeled off her soaking jacket. "We'll need a vase for the flowers, Cards. They're for Mr. Haines's room. Make sure Jamie's not about, will you?"

"Naturally, Miss." Cards took both the dripping jackets and the dripping flowers and headed back down the hall.

"Where'd you find him?" Adam wondered aloud. "He's incredible."

"Cards?" Like a wet dog, Kirby shook her head. "Papa brought him back from England. I think he was a spy, or maybe it was a bouncer. In either case, it's obvious he's seen everything."

"Well, children, have you had a nice holiday?" Fairchild bounced out of the parlor. He wore a paint-streaked shirt and a smug smile. "My work's complete, and now I'm free to give my full attention to my sculpting. It's time I called Victor Alvarez," he murmured. "I've kept him dangling long enough."

"He'll dangle until after coffee, Papa." She sent her father a quick warning glance Adam might've missed if he hadn't been watching so closely. "Take Adam in the parlor and I'll see to it."

She kept him occupied for the rest of the day. Deliberately, Adam realized. Something was going on that she didn't want him getting an inkling of. Over dinner, she was again the perfect hostess. Over coffee and brandy in the parlor, she kept him entertained with an in-depth discussion on baroque art. Though her conversations and charm were effortless, Adam was certain there was an underlying reason. It was one more thing for him to discover.

She couldn't have set the scene better, he mused. A quiet parlor, a crackling fire, intelligent conversation. And she was watching Fairchild like a hawk.

When Montique entered, the scene changed. Once again, the scruffy puppy leaped into Adam's lap and settled down.

"How the hell did he get in here?" Fairchild demanded.

"Adam encourages him," Kirby stated as she sipped at her brandy. "We can't be held responsible."

"I should say not!" Fairchild gave both Adam and Montique a steely look. "And if that—that creature threatens to sue again, Adam will have to retain his own attorney. I won't be involved in a legal battle, particularly when I have my business with Señor Alvarez to complete. What time is it in Brazil?''

"Some time or other," Kirby murmured.

"I'll call him immediately and close the deal before we find ourselves slapped with a summons."

Adam sat back with his brandy and scratched Montique's ears. "You two don't seriously expect me to believe you're worried about being sued by a cat?"

Kirby ran a fingertip around the rim of her snifter. "I don't think we'd better tell him about what happened last year when we tried to have her evicted."

"No!" Fairchild leaped up and shuffled before he darted to the door. "I won't discuss it. I won't remember it. I'm going to call Brazil."

"Ah, Adam . . ." Kirby trailed off with a meaningful glance at the doorway.

Adam didn't have to look to know that Isabelle was making an entrance.

"I won't be intimidated by a cat."

"I'm sure that's very stalwart of you." Kirby downed the rest of her drink then rose. "Just as I'm sure you'll understand if I leave you to your courage. I really have to reline my dresser drawers."

For the second time that day, Adam found himself alone with a dog and cat.

A half hour later, after he'd lost a staring match with Isabelle, Adam locked his door and contacted McIntyre. In the brief, concise tones that McIntyre had always admired, Adam relayed the conversation he'd overheard the night before.

"It fits," McIntyre stated. Adam could almost see him rubbing his hands together. "You've learned quite a bit in a short time. The check on Hiller reveals he's living on credit and reputation. Both are running thin. No idea where Fairchild's keeping it?''

"I'm surprised he doesn't have it hanging in full view." Adam lit a cigarette and frowned at the Titian across the room. "It would be just like him. He mentioned a Victor Alvarez from Brazil a couple of times. Some kind of deal he's cooking."

"I'll see what I can dig up. Maybe he's selling the Rembrandt."

"He hardly needs the money."

"Some people never have enough."

"Yeah." But it didn't fit. It just didn't fit. "I'll get back to you."

Adam brooded, but only for a few moments. The sooner he had something tangible, the sooner he could untangle himself. He opened the panel and went to work.

In the morning Kirby posed for Adam for more than two hours without the slightest argument. If he thought her cooperation and her sunny disposition were designed to confuse him, he was absolutely right. She was also keeping him occupied while Fairchild made the final arrangements for the disposal of the Van Gogh.

Adam had worked the night before until after midnight, but had found nothing. Wherever Fairchild had hidden the Rembrandt, he'd hidden it well. Adam's search of the third floor was almost complete. It was time to look elsewhere.

"Hidden with respect and affection," he remembered. In all probability that would rule out the dungeons and the attic. Chances were he'd have to give them some time, but he intended to concentrate on the main portion of the house first. His main objective would be Fairchild's private rooms, but when and how he'd do them he had yet to determine.

After the painting session was over and Kirby went back to her own work, Adam wandered around the first floor. There was no one to question his presence. He was a guest and he was trusted. He was supposed to be, he reminded himself when he became uncomfortable. One of the reasons McIntyre had drafted him for this particular job was because he would have easy access to the Fairchilds and the house. He was, socially and professionally, one of them. They'd have no reason to be suspicious of a well-bred, successful artist whom they'd welcomed into their own home. And the more Adam tried to justify his actions, the more the guilt ate at him.

Enough, he told himself as he stared out at the darkening sky. He'd had enough for one day. It was time he went up and changed for Melanie Burgess's party. There he'd meet Stuart Hiller and Harriet Merrick. There was no emotional ties there to make him feel like a spy and a thief. Swearing at himself, he started up the stairs.

"Excuse me, Mr. Haines." Impatient, Adam turned and looked down at Tulip. "Were you going up?"

"Yes." Because he stood on the bottom landing blocking her way, he stood aside to let her pass.

"You take this up to her then, and see she drinks it." Tulip shoved a tall glass of milky white liquid into his hand. "All," she added tersely before she clomped back toward the kitchen.

Where did they get their servants, Adam wondered, frowning down at the glass in his hands. And why, for the love of God had he let himself be ordered around by one? When in Rome, he supposed, and started up the steps again.

The *she* obviously meant Kirby. Adam sniffed doubtfully at the glass as he knocked on her door.

"You can bring it in," she called out, "but I won't drink it. Threaten all you like."

All right, he decided and pushed her door open. The bedroom was empty, but he could smell her.

"Do your worst," she invited. "You can't intimidate me with stories of intestinal disorders and vitamin deficiencies. I'm healthy as a horse."

The warm, sultry scent flowed over him. Glass in hand, he walked through and into the bathroom where the steam rose up, fragrant and misty as a rain forest. With her hair pinned on top of her head, Kirby lounged in a huge sunken tub. Overhead, hanging plants dripped down, green and moist. White frothy bubbles floated in heaps on the surface of the water.

"So she sent you, did she?" Unconcerned, Kirby rubbed a loofah sponge over one shoulder. The bubbles, she concluded, covered her with more modesty than most woman at the party that night would claim. "Well, come in then and stop scowling at me. I won't ask you to scrub my back."

He thought of Cleopatra, floating on her barge. Just how many men other than Caesar and Antony had she driven mad? He glanced at the long mirrored wall behind the sink. It was fogged with the steam that rose in visible columns from her bath. "Got the water hot enough?"

"Do you know what that is?" she demanded and plucked her soap from the dish. The cake was a pale, pale pink and left a creamy lather on her skin. "It's a filthy-tasting mixture Tulip tries to force on me periodically. It has raw eggs in it and other vile things." Making a face she lifted one surprisingly long leg out of the bath and soaped it. "Tell me the truth, Adam, would you voluntarily drink raw eggs?"

He watched her run soap and fingertips down her calf. "I can't say I would."

"Well, then." Satisfied, she switched legs. "Down the drain with it."

"She told me to see that you drank it. All," he added, beginning to enjoy himself.

Her lower lip moved forward a bit as she considered. "Puts you in an awkward position, doesn't it?"

"A position in any case."

"Tell you what, I'll have a sip. Then when she asks if I drank it I can say I did. I'm trying to cut down on my lying."

Adam handed her the glass, watching as she sipped and grimaced. "I'm not sure you're being truthful this way."

"I said cutting down, not eliminating. Into the sink," she added. "Unless you'd care for the rest."

"I'll pass." He poured it out then sat on the lip of the tub.

Surprised by the move, she tightened her fingers on the soap. It plopped into the water. "Hydrophobia," she muttered. "No, don't bother, I'll find it." Dipping her hand in, she began to search. "You'd think they could make a soap that wasn't forever leaping out of your hands." Grateful for the distraction, she gripped the soap again. "Aha. I appreciate your bringing me that revolting stuff, Adam. Now if you'd like to run along . . ."

"I'm in no hurry." Idly he picked up her loofah. "You mentioned something about scrubbing your back."

"Robbery!" Fairchild's voice boomed into the room just ahead of him. "Call the police. Call the FBI. Adam, you'll be a witness." He nodded, finding nothing odd in the audience to his daughter's bath.

"I'm so glad I have a large bathroom," she murmured. "Pity I didn't think to serve refreshments." Relieved by the interruption she ran the soap down her arm. "What's been stolen, Papa? The Monet street scene, the Renoir portrait? I know, your sweat socks."

"My black dinner suit!" Dramatically he pointed a finger to the ceiling. "We'll have to take fingerprints."

"Obviously stolen by a psychotic with a fetish for formal attire," Kirby concluded. "I love a mystery. Let's list the suspects." She pushed a lock of hair out of her eyes and leaned back—a naked, erotic Sherlock Holmes. "Adam, have you an alibi?"

With a half smile, he ran the damp abrasive sponge through his hands. "I've been seducing Polly all afternoon."

Her eyes lit with amusement. She'd known he had potential. "That won't do," she said soberly. "It wouldn't take above fifteen minutes to seduce Polly. You have a black dinner suit, I suppose."

"Circumstantial evidence."

"A search warrant," Fairchild chimed in, inspired. "We'll get a search warrant and go through the entire house."

"Time-consuming," Kirby decided. "Actually, Papa, I think we'd best look to Cards."

"The butler did it." Fairchild cackled with glee, then immediately sobered. "No, no, my suit would never fit Cards."

"True. Still, as much as I hate to be an informer, I overheard Cards telling Tulip he intended to take your suit."

"Trust," Fairchild mumbled to Adam. "Can't trust anyone."

"His motive was sponging and pressing, I believe." She sunk down to her neck and examined her toes. "He'll crumble like a wall if you accuse him. I'm sure of it."

"Very well." Fairchild rubbed his thin, clever hands together. "I'll handle it myself and avoid the publicity."

"A brave man," Kirby decided as her father strode out of the room. Relaxed and amused, she smiled at Adam. "Well, my bubbles seem to be melting so we'd better continue this discussion some other time."

Reaching over, Adam yanked the chain and drew the old-fashioned plug out of the stupendous tub. "The time's coming when we're going to start—and finish—much more than a conversation."

Wary, Kirby watched her water level and last defense recede. When cornered, she determined, it was best to be nonchalant. She tried a smile that didn't quite conceal the nerves. "Let me know when you're ready."

"I intend to," he said softly. Without another word, he rose and left her alone.

Later, when he descended the stairs, Adam grinned when he heard her voice.

"Yes, Tulip, I drank the horrid stuff. I won't disgrace you by fainting in the Merrick living room from malnutrition." The low rumble of response that followed was dissatisfied. "Cricket wings, I've been walking in heels for half my life. They're not six inches, they're three. And I'll still have to look up at everyone over twelve. Go bake a cake, will you?"

He heard Tulip's mutter and sniff before she stomped out of the room and passed him.

"Adam, thank God. Let's go before she finds something else to nag me about."

Her dress was pure unadorned white, thin and floaty. It covered her arms, rose high at the throat, as modest as a nun's habit, as sultry as a tropical night. Her hair fell, black and straight over the shoulders.

Tossing it back, she picked up a black cape and swirled it around her. For a moment she stood, adjusting it while the light from the lamps flitted over the absence of color. She looked like a Manet portrait— strong, romantic and timeless.

"You're a fabulous-looking creature, Kirby."

They both stopped, staring. He'd given compliments before, with more style, more finesse, but he'd never meant one more. She'd been flattered by princes, in foreign tongues and with smooth deliveries. It had never made her stomach flutter.

"Thank you," she managed. "So're you." No longer sure it was wise, she offered her hand. "Are you ready?"

"Yes. Your father?"

"He's already gone," she told him as she walked toward the door. And the sooner they were, the better. She needed a little more time before she was alone with him again. "We don't drive to parties together, especially to Harriet's. He likes to get there early and usually stays longer, trying to talk Harriet into bed. I've had my car brought around." She shut the door and led him to a silver Porsche. "I'd rather drive than navigate, if you don't mind."

But she didn't wait for his response as she dropped into the driver's seat. "Fine," Adam agreed.

"It's a marvelous night." She turned the key in the ignition. The power vibrated under their feet. "Full moon, lots of stars." Smoothly she released the brake, engaged the clutch and pressed the accelerator. Adam was tossed against the seat as they roared down the drive.

"You'll like Harriet," Kirby continued, switching gears as Adam stared at the blurring landscape. "She's like a mother to me." When they came to the main road, Kirby downshifted and swung to the left, tires squealing. "You met Melly, of course. I hope you won't desert me completely tonight after seeing her again."

Adam braced his feet against the floor. "Does anyone notice her when you're around?" And would they make it to the Merrick home alive?

"Of course." Surprised by the question, she turned to look at him.

"Good God, watch where you're going!" None too gently, he pushed her head around.

"Melly's the most perfectly beautiful woman I've ever known." Downshifting again, Kirby squealed around a right turn then accelerated. "She's a very clever designer and very, very proper. Wouldn't even take a settlement from her husband when they divorced. Pride, I suppose, but then she wouldn't need the money. There's a marvelous view of the Hudson coming up on your side, Adam." Kirby leaned over to point it out. The car swerved.

"I prefer seeing it from up here, thanks," Adam told her as he shoved her back in her seat. "Do you always drive this way?"

"Yes. There's the road you take to the gallery," she continued. She waved her hand vaguely as the car whizzed by an intersection. Adam glanced down at the speedometer.

"You're doing ninety."

"I always drive slower at night."

"There's good news." Muttering, he flicked on the lighter.

"There's the house up ahead." She raced around an ess curve. "Fabulous when it's all lit up this way."

The house was white and stately, the type you expected to see high above the riverbank. It glowed with elegance from dozens of windows. Without slackening pace, Kirby sped up the circular drive. With a squeal of brakes, and a muttered curse from Adam, she stopped the Porsche at the front entrance.

Reaching over, Adam pulled the keys from the ignition and pocketed them. "I'm driving back."

"How thoughtful." Offering her hand to the valet, Kirby stepped out. "Now I won't have to limit myself to one drink. Champagne," she decided, moving up the steps beside him. "It seems like a night for it."

The moment the door opened, Kirby was enveloped by a flurry of dazzling, trailing silks. "Harriet." Kirby squeezed the statuesque woman with flaming red hair. "It's wonderful to see you but I think I'm being gnawed by the denture work of your crocodile."

"Sorry, darling." Harriet held her necklace and drew back to press a kiss to each of Kirby's cheeks. She was an impressive woman, full-bodied in the style Rubens had immortalized. Her face was wide and smooth, dominated by deep green eyes that glittered with silver on the lids. Harriet didn't believe in subtlety. "And this must be your houseguest," she continued with a quick sizing up of Adam.

"Harriet Merrick, Adam Haines." Kirby grinned and pinched Harriet's cheek. "And behave yourself or Papa'll have him choosing weapons."

"Wonderful idea." With one arm still linked with Kirby's, Harriet twined her other through Adam's. "I'm sure you have a fascinating life story to tell me, Adam."

"I'll make one up."

"Perfect." She liked the look of him. "We've a crowd already, though they're mostly Melanie's stuffy friends."

"Harriet, you've got to be more tolerant."

"No, I don't." She tossed back her outrageous hair. "I've been excrutiatingly polite. Now that you're here, I don't have to be."

"Kirby." Melanie swept into the hall in an ice-blue sheath. "What a picture you make. Take her cloak, Ellen, though it's a pity to spoil that effect." Smiling, she held out a hand to Adam as the maid slipped Kirby's cloak off her shoulders. "I'm so glad you came. We've some mutual acquaintances here, it seems. The Birminghams and Michael Towers from New York. You remember Michael, Kirby?"

"The adman who clicks his teeth?"

Harriet let out a roar of laughter while Adam struggled to control his. With a sigh, Melanie led them toward the party. "Try to behave, will you?" But Adam wasn't certain whether she spoke to Kirby or her mother.

This was the world he was used to—elegant people in elegant clothes having rational conversations. He'd been raised in the world of restrained wealth where champagne fizzed quietly and dignity was as essential as the proper alma mater. He understood it, he fit in.

After fifteen minutes, he was separated from Kirby and bored to death.

"I've decided to take a trek through the Australian bush," Harriet told Kirby. She fingered her necklace of crocodile teeth. "I'd love you to come with me. We'd have such fun brewing a billy cup over the fire."

"Camping?" Kirby asked, mulling it over. Maybe what she needed was a change of scene, after her father settled down.

"Give it some thought," Harriet suggested. "I'm not planning on leaving for another six weeks. Ah, Adam." Reaching out, she grabbed his arm. "Did Agnes Birmingham drive you to drink? No, don't an-

First Class Romance

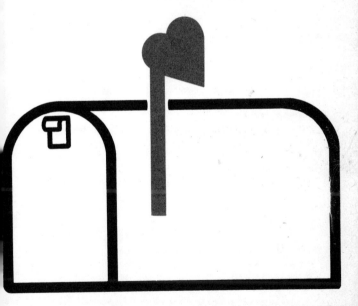

Delivered to your door by

Silhouette Intimate Moments®

Find romance at your door with 4 FREE Silhouette Intimate Moments novels!

Now you can have the intense romances you crave without searching for them. You can receive Silhouette Intimate Moments novels, each month, to read in your own home.

Silhouette Intimate Moments is a series written for women—not for girls. These are stories about our times, when men and women's lives are ablaze with passion and explosive desires.

You can share in the power and abandon of their love, every month, beginning with 4 new Silhouette Intimate Moments novels. Worth $10.00, these romances are yours FREE, along with a Cameo Tote Bag.

By filling out and mailing the attached postage-paid order card, you'll also receive an extra bonus: our monthly Silhouette Books Newsletter.

Approximately every 4 weeks, we'll send you four more Silhouette Intimate Moments novels to examine FREE for 15 days. If you decide to keep them, you'll pay just $9.00— with no extra charge for home delivery and at no risk! You'll also have the option of cancelling at anytime. Just drop us a note. Your first 4 books and the Tote Bag are yours to keep in any case.

Silhouette Intimate Moments ®

EXTRA BONUS
A Free Cameo Tote

You'll receive brand-new novels as they're published!

Mail this card today for your
4 FREE BOOKS
and this Tote Bag
(a $16.99 value)!

swer. It's written all over your face, but you're much too polite."

He allowed himself to be drawn between her and Kirby, where he wanted to be. "Let's just say I was looking for more stimulating conversation. I've found it."

"Charming." She decided she liked him, but would reserve judgment a bit longer as to whether he'd suit her Kirby. "I admire your work, Adam. I'd like to put the first bid in on your next painting."

He took glasses from a passing waiter. "I'm doing a portrait of Kirby."

"She's posing for you?" Harriet nearly choked on her champagne. "Did you chain her?"

"Not yet." He gave Kirby a lazy glance. "It's still a possibility."

"You have to let me display it when it's finished." She might've been a woman who ran on emotion on many levels, but the bottom line was art, and the business of it. "I can promise to cause a nasty scene if you refuse."

"No one does it better," Kirby toasted her.

"You'll have to see the portrait of Kirby that Philip painted for me. She wouldn't sit for it, but it's brilliant." She toyed with the stem of her glass. "He painted it when she returned from Paris—three years ago, I suppose."

"I'd like to see it. I'd planned on coming by the gallery."

"Oh, it's here, in the library."

"Why don't you two just toddle along then," Kirby suggested. "You've been talking around me, you might as well desert me physically as well."

"Don't be snotty," Harriet told her. "You can come, too. And I . . . Well, well," she murmured in a voice suddenly lacking in warmth. "Some people have no sense of propriety."

Kirby turned her head, just slightly, and watched Stuart walk into the room. Her fingers tightened on the glass, but she shrugged. Before the movement was complete, Melanie was at her side.

"I'm sorry, Kirby. I'd hoped he wouldn't come after all."

In a slow, somehow insolent gesture, Kirby pushed her hair behind her back. "If it had mattered, I wouldn't have come."

"I don't want you to be embarrassed," Melanie began only to be cut off by a quick and very genuine laugh.

"When have you ever known me to be embarrassed?"

"Well, I'll greet him, or it'll make matters worse." Still Melanie hesitated, obviously torn between loyalty and manners.

"I'll fire him, of course," Harriet mused when her daughter went to do her duty. "But I want to be subtle about it."

"Fire him if you like, Harriet, but not on my account." Kirby drained her champagne.

"It appears we're in for a show, Adam." Harriet tapped a coral fingertip against her glass. "Much to Melanie's distress, Stuart's coming over."

Without saying a word, Kirby took Adam's cigarette.

"Harriet, you look marvelous." The smooth, cultured voice wasn't at all like the tone Adam had heard in Fairchild's studio. "Africa agreed with you."

Harriet gave him a bland smile. "We didn't expect to see you."

"I was tied up for a bit." Charming, elegant, he turned to Kirby. "You're looking lovely."

"So are you," she said evenly. "It seems your nose is back in joint." Without missing a beat, she turned to Adam. "I don't believe you've met. Adam, this is Stuart Hiller. I'm sure you know Adam Haines's work, Stuart."

"Yes, indeed." The handshake was polite and meaningless. "Are you staying in our part of New York long?"

"Until I finish Kirby's portrait," Adam told him and had the dual satisfaction of seeing Kirby grin and Stuart frown. "I've agreed to let Harriet display it in the gallery."

With that simple strategy, Adam won Harriet over.

"I'm sure it'll be a tremendous addition to our collection." Even a man with little sensitivity wouldn't have missed the waves of resentment. For the moment Stuart ignored them. "I wasn't able to reach you in Africa, Harriet, and thing's have been hectic since your return. The Titian woman has been sold to Ernest Myerling."

As he lifted his glass, Adam's attention focused on Kirby. Her color drained, slowly, degree by degree until her face was as white as the silk she wore.

"I don't recall discussing selling the Titian," Harriet countered. Her voice was as colorless as Kirby's skin.

"As I said, I couldn't reach you. As the Titian isn't listed under your personal collection, it falls among the saleable paintings. I think you'll be pleased with the price." He lit a cigarette with a slim silver lighter. "Myerling did insist on having it tested. He's more interested in investment than art, I'm afraid. I thought you'd want to be there tomorrow for the procedure."

Oh, God, oh, my God! Panic, very real and very strong whirled through Kirby's mind. In silence Adam watched the fear grow in her eyes.

"Tested!" Obviously insulted, Harriet seethed. "Of all the gall, doubting the authenticity of a painting from my gallery. The Titian should not have been sold without my permission, and certainly not to a peasant."

"Testing isn't unheard of, Harriet." Seeing a hefty commission wavering, Stuart soothed, "Myerling's a businessman, not an art expert. He wants facts." Taking a long drag, he blew out smoke. "In any case, the paperwork's already completed and there's nothing to be done about it. The deal's a fait accompli, hinging on the test results."

"We'll discuss this in the morning." Harriet's voice lowered as she finished off her drink. "This isn't the time or place."

"I—I have to freshen my drink," Kirby said suddenly. Without another word, she spun away to work her way through the crowd. The nausea, she realized, was a direct result of panic, and the panic was a long way from over. "Papa." She latched onto his arm and pulled him out of a discussion on Dali's versatility. "I have to talk to you. Now."

Hearing the edge in her voice, he let her drag him from the room.

Chapter 7

Kirby closed the doors of Harriet's library behind her and leaned back against them. She didn't waste any time. "The Titian's being tested in the morning. Stuart sold it."

"Sold it!" Fairchild's eyes grew wide, his face pink. "Impossible. Harriet wouldn't sell the Titian."

"She didn't. She was off playing with lions, remember?" Dragging both hands through her hair, she tried to speak calmly. "Stuart closed the deal, he just told her."

"I told you he was a fool, didn't I? Didn't I?" Fairchild repeated as he started dancing in place. "I told Harriet, too. Would anyone listen? No, not Harriet." He whirled around, plucked up a pencil from her desk and broke it in two. "She hires the idiot anyway and goes off to roam the jungle."

"There's no use going over that again!" Kirby snapped at him. "We've got to deal with the results."

"There wouldn't be any results if I'd been listened to. Stubborn woman falling for a pretty face. That's all it was." Pausing, he took a deep breath and folded his hands. "Well," he said in a mild voice, "this is a problem."

"Papa, this isn't an error in your checkbook."

"But it can be handled, probably with less effort. Any way out of the deal?"

"Stuart said the paperwork had been finalized. And it's Myerling," she added.

"That old pirate." He scowled a moment and gave Harriet's desk a quick kick. "No way out of it," Fairchild concluded. "On to the next step. We exchange them." He saw by Kirby's nod she'd already thought of it. There was a quick flash of pride before anger set in. The round, cherubic face tightened. "By God, Stuart's going to pay for making me give up that painting."

"Very easily said, Papa." Kirby walked into the room until she stood toe to toe with him. "But who was it who settled Adam in the same room with the painting? Now we're going to have to get it out of his room, then get the copy from the gallery in without him knowing there's been a switch. I'm sure you've noticed Adam's not a fool."

Fairchild's eyebrows wiggled. His lips curved. He rubbed his palms together. "A plan."

Knowing it was too late for regrets, Kirby flopped into a chair. "We'll phone Cards and have him put the painting in my room before we get back."

He approved this with a brief nod. "You have a marvelous criminal mind, Kirby."

She had to smile. A sense of adventure was already spearing through the panic. "Heredity," she told her father. "Now, here's my idea...." Lowering her voice, she began the outline.

"It'll work," Fairchild decided a few moments later.

"That has yet to be seen." It sounded plausible enough, but she didn't underestimate Adam Haines. "So there's nothing to be done but to do it."

"And do it well."

Her agreement was a careless shrug of her shoulders. "Adam should be too tired to notice that the Titian's gone, and after I make the exchange at the gallery, I'll slip it back into his room. Sleeping pills are the only way." She stared down at her hands, dissatisfied, but knowing it was the only way out. "I don't like doing this to Adam."

"He'll just get a good night's sleep." Fairchild sat on the arm of her chair. "We all need a good night's sleep now and again. Now we'd better go back or Melanie'll send out search parties."

"You go first." Kirby let out a deep breath. "I'll phone Cards and tell him to get started."

Kirby waited until Fairchild had closed the doors again before she went to the phone on Harriet's desk. She didn't mind the job she had to do, in fact, she looked forward to it. Except for Adam's part. It couldn't be helped, she reminded herself and gave Cards brief instructions.

Now, she thought as she replaced the receiver, it was too late to turn back. The die, so to speak, had been cast. The truth was, the hastily made plans for the evening would prove a great deal more interesting than a party. While she hesitated a moment longer, Stuart opened the door, then closed it softly behind him.

"Kirby." He crossed to her with a half smile on his face. His patience had paid off now that he'd found her alone. "We have to talk."

Not now, she thought on a moment's panic. Didn't she have enough to deal with? Then she thought of the way he'd humiliated her. They way he'd lied. Perhaps it was better to get everything over with at once.

"I think we said everything we had to say at our last meeting."

"Not nearly everything."

"Redundance bores me," she said mildly. "But if you insist, I'll say this. It's a pity you haven't the money to suit your looks. Your mistake, Stuart, was in not making me want you—not the way you wanted me." Deliberately her voice dropped, low and seductive. She hadn't nearly finished paying him back. "You could deceive me about love, but not about lust. If you'd concentrated on that instead of greed, you might've had a chance. You are," she continued softly, "a liar and a cheat, and while that might've been an interesting diversion for a short time, I thank God you never got your hands on me or my money."

Before she could sweep around him, he grabbed her arm. "You'd better remember your father's habits before you sling mud."

She dropped her gaze to his hand then slowly raised it again. It was a look designed to infuriate. "Do you honestly compare yourself with my father?" Her fury came out on a laugh and the laugh was insult itself.

"You'll never have his style, Stuart. You're second rate, and you'll always be second rate."

He brought the back of his hand across her face hard enough to make her stagger. She didn't make a sound. When she stared up at him, her eyes were slits, very dark, very dangerous slits. The pain meant nothing, only that he'd caused it and she had no way to pay him back in kind. Yet.

"You prove my point," Kirby said evenly as she brushed her fingers over her cheek. "Second rate."

He wanted to hit her again, but balled his hands into fists. He needed her, for the moment. "I'm through playing games, Kirby. I want the Rembrandt."

"I'd take a knife to it before I saw Papa hand it over to you. You're out of your class, Stuart." She didn't bother to struggle when he grabbed her arms.

"Two days, Kirby. You tell the old man he has two days or it's you who'll pay."

"Threats and physical abuse are your only weapons." Abruptly, with more effort that she allowed him to see, Kirby turned her anger to ice. "I've weapons of my own, Stuart, infinitely more effective. And if I chose to drop to gutter tactics, you haven't the finesse to deal with me." She kept her eyes on his, her body still. He might curse her, but Stuart knew the truth when he heard it. "You're a snake," she added quietly. "And you can't stay off your belly for long. The fact that you're stronger than I is only a temporary advantage."

"Very temporary," Adam said as he closed the door at his back. His voice matched Kirby's chill for chill. "Take your hands off her."

Kirby felt the painful grip on her arms relax and watched Stuart struggle with composure. Carefully he straightened his tie. "Remember what I said, Kirby. It could be important to you."

"You remember how Byron described a woman's revenge," she countered as she rubbed the circulation back into her arm. "'Like a tiger's spring—deadly, quick and crushing.'" She dropped her arms to her sides. "It could be important to you." Turning, she walked to the window and stared out at nothing.

Adam kept his hand on the knob as Stuart walked to the door. "Touch her again and you'll have to deal with me." Slowly Adam turned the knob and opened the door. "That's something else for you to remember." The sounds of the party flowed in then silenced again as he shut the door at Stuart's back.

"Well," he began, struggling with his own fury. "I guess I should be grateful I don't have an ex-fiancé hanging around." He'd heard enough to know that the Rembrandt had been at the bottom of it, but he pushed that aside and went to her. "He's a poor loser, and you're amazing. Most women would have been weeping or pleading. You stood there flinging insults."

"I don't believe in pleading," she said as lightly as she could. "And Stuart would never reduce me to tears."

"But you're trembling," he murmured as he put his hands on her shoulders.

"Anger." She drew in a deep breath and let it out slowly. She didn't care to show a weakness, not to anyone. "I appreciate the white knight routine."

He grinned and kissed the top of her head. "Any time. Why don't we..." He trailed off as he turned her to face him. The mark of Stuart's hand had faded to a dull angry red, but it was unmistakable. When Adam touched his fingers to her cheek, his eyes were cold. Colder and more dangerous than she'd ever seen them. Without a word, he spun around and headed for the door.

"No!" Desperation wasn't characteristic, but she felt it now as she grabbed his arm. "No, Adam, don't. Don't get involved." He shook her off, but she sprinted to the door ahead of him and stood with her back pressed against it. The tears she'd been able to control with Stuart now swam in her eyes. "Please, I've enough on my conscience without dragging you into this. I live my life as I choose, and what I get from it is of my own making."

He wanted to brush her aside and push through the crowd outside the door until he had his hands on Stuart. He wanted, more than he'd ever wanted anything, the pleasure of smelling the other man's blood. But she was standing in front of him, small and delicate, with tears in her eyes. She wasn't the kind of woman tears came easily to.

"All right." He brushed one from her cheek and made a promise on it. Before it was over, he would indeed smell Stuart Hiller's blood. "You're only postponing the inevitable."

Relieved, she closed her eyes a moment. When she opened them again, they were still damp but no longer desperate. "I don't believe in the inevitable." She took his hand and brought it to her cheek, holding it there a moment until she felt the tension drain from both of them. "You must've come in to see my portrait. It's there, above the desk."

She gestured, but he didn't take his eyes from hers. "I'll give it a thorough study, right after I give my attention to the original." He gathered her close and just held her. It was, though neither one of them had known it, the most perfect gesture of support. Resting her head against his shoulder, she thought of peace, and she thought of the plans that had already been put into motion.

"I'm sorry, Adam."

He heard the regret in her voice and brushed his lips over her hair. "What for?"

"I can't tell you." She tightened her arms around his waist and clung to him as she had never clung to anyone. "But I am sorry."

The drive away from the Merrick estate was more sedate than the approach. Kirby sat in the passenger seat. Under most circumstances, Adam would've attributed her silence and unease to her scene with Hiller. But he remembered her reaction at the mention of the sale of a Titian.

What was going on in that kaleidoscope brain of hers? he wondered. And how was he going to find out? The direct approach, Adam decided and thought fleetingly that it was a shame to waste the moonlight. "The Titian that's been sold," he began, pretending he didn't see Kirby jolt. "Has Harriet had it long?"

"The Titian." She folded her hands in her lap. "Oh, years and years. Your Mrs. Birmingham's shaped like a zucchini, don't you think?"

"She's not my Mrs. Birmingham." A new game, he concluded and relaxed against the seat. "It's too bad it was sold before I could see it. I'm a great admirer of Titian. The painting in my room's exquisite."

Kirby let out a sound that might have been a nervous giggle. "The one at the gallery is just as exquisite," she told him. "Ah, here we are, home again. Just leave the car out front," she said, half relieved, half annoyed that the next steps were being put into play. "Cards will see to it. I hope you don't mind coming back early, Adam. There's Papa," she added as she stepped from the car. "He must've struck out with Harriet. Let's have a nightcap, shall we?"

She started up the steps without waiting for his agreement. Knowing he was about to become a part of some hastily conceived plan, he went along. It's all too pat, he mused as Fairchild waited at the door with a genial smile.

"Too many people," Fairchild announced. "I much prefer small parties. Let's have a drink in the parlor and gossip."

Don't look so bloody anxious, Kirby thought and nearly scowled at him. "I'll go tell Cards to see to the Rolls and my car." Still, she hesitated as the men walked toward the parlor. Adam caught the indecision in her eyes before Fairchild cackled and slapped him on the back.

"And don't hurry back," he told Kirby. "I've had enough of women for a while."

"How sweet." The irony and strength came back into her voice. "I'll just go in and eat Tulip's lemon trifle. All," she added as she swept past.

Fairchild thought of his midnight snack with regret. "Brat," he muttered. "Well, we'll have scotch instead."

Adam dipped his hands casually in his pockets and watched every move Fairchild made. "I had a chance to see Kirby's portrait in Harriet's library. It's marvelous."

"One of my best, if I say so myself." Fairchild lifted the decanter of Chivas Regal. "Harriet's fond of my brat, you know." In a deft move, Fairchild slipped two pills from his pocket and dropped them into the scotch.

Under normal circumstances Adam would've missed it. Clever hands, he thought as intrigued as he was amused. Very quick, very agile. Apparently they wanted him out of the way. He was going to find it a challenge to pit himself against both of them. With a smile, he accepted the drink then turned to the Corot landscape behind him.

"Carot's treatment of light," Adam began, taking a small sip. "It gives all of his work such deep perspective."

No ploy could've worked better. Fairchild was ready to roll. "I'm very partial to Corot. He had such a fine hand with details without being finicky and obscuring the overall painting. Now the leaves," he began and set down his drink to point them out. While the lecture went on, Adam set down his own drink, picked up Fairchild's and enjoyed the scotch.

Upstairs Kirby found the Titian already wrapped in heavy paper. "Bless you, Cards," she murmured. She checked her watch and made herself wait a full ten minutes before she picked up the painting and left the room. Quietly she moved down the back stairs and out to where her car waited.

In the parlor, Adam studied Fairchild as he sat in the corner of the sofa, snoring. Deciding the least he could do was to make his host more comfortable, Adam started to swing Fairchild's legs onto the couch. The sound of a car engine stopped him. Adam was at the window in time to see Kirby's Porsche race down the drive.

"You're going to have company," he promised her. Within moments, he was behind the wheel of the Rolls.

The surge of speed added to Kirby's sense of adventure. She drove instinctively while she concentrated on her task for the evening. It helped ease the guilt over Adam, a bit.

A quarter mile from the gallery, she stopped and parked on the side of the road. Grateful that the Titian was relatively small, though the frame added weight, she gathered it up again and began to walk. Her heels echoed on the asphalt.

Clouds drifted across the moon, obscuring the light then freeing it again. With her cape swirling around her, Kirby walked into the cover of trees that bordered the gallery. The light was dim, all shadows and secrets. Up ahead came the low moan of an owl. Tossing back her hair, she laughed.

"Perfect," she decided. "All we need is a rumble of thunder and a few streaks of lightning. Skulking through the woods on a desperate mission," she mused. "Surrounded by the sounds of night." She shifted the bundle in her arms and continued on. "What one does for those one loves."

She could see the stately red brick of the gallery through the trees. Moonlight slanted over it. Almost there, she thought with a quick glance at her watch. In an hour she'd be back home—and perhaps she'd have the lemon trifle after all.

A hand fell heavily on her shoulder. Her cape spread out like wings as she whirled. Great buckets of blood, she thought as she stared up at Adam.

"Out for a stroll?" he asked her.

"Why hello, Adam." Since she couldn't disappear, she had to face him down. She tried a friendly smile. "What are you doing out here?"

"Following you."

"Flattering. But wasn't Papa entertaining you?"

"He dozed off."

She stared up at him a moment, then let out a breath. A wry smile followed it. "I suppose he deserved it; I hope you left him comfortable."

"Enough. Now what's in the package?"

Though she knew it was useless, she fluttered her lashes. "Package?"

He tapped his finger on the wrapping.

"Oh, this package. Just a little errand I have to run. It's getting late, shouldn't you be starting back?"

"Not a chance."

"No." She moved her shoulders. "I thought not."

"What's in the package, Kirby, and what do you intend to do with it?"

"All right." She thrust the painting into his arms because hers were tiring. When the jig was up, you had to make the best of it. "I suppose you deserve an explanation, and you won't leave until you have one anyway. It has to be the condensed version, Adam,

I'm running behind schedule." She laid a hand on the package he held. "This is the Titian woman and I'm going to put it in the gallery."

He lifted a brow. He didn't need Kirby to tell him that he held a painting. "I was under the impression that the Titian woman was in the gallery."

"No..." She drew out the word. If she could have thought of a lie, a half truth, a fable, she'd have used it. She could only think of the truth. "This is a Titian," she told him with a nod to the package. "The painting in the gallery is a Fairchild."

He let the silence hang a moment while the moonlight filtered over her face. She looked like an angel... or a witch. "Your father forged a Titian and palmed it off on the gallery as an original?"

"Certainly not!" Indignation wasn't feigned. Kirby bit back on it and tried to be patient. "I won't tell you any more if you insult my father."

"I don't know what came over me."

"All right then." She leaned back against a tree. "Perhaps I should start at the beginning."

"Good choice."

"Years ago, Papa and Harriet were vacationing in Europe. They came across the Titian, each one swearing they'd seen it first. Neither one would give way, and it would've been criminal to let the painting go altogether. They compromised." She gestured at the package. "Each paid half and Papa painted a copy. They rotate ownership of the original every six months, alternating with the copy, if you get the drift. The stipulation was that neither of them could claim ownership. Harriet kept hers in the gallery—not listing it as part of her private collection. Papa kept it in a guest room.''

He considered for a moment. ''That's too ridiculous for you to have made up.''

''Of course I didn't make it up.'' As it could, effectively, her bottom lip pouted. ''Don't you trust me?''

''No. You're going to do a lot more explaining when we get back.''

Perhaps, Kirby thought. And perhaps not.

''Now just how do you intend to get into the gallery?''

''With Harriet's keys.''

''She gave you her keys?''

Kirby let out a frustrated breath. ''Pay attention, Adam. Harriet's furious about Stuart selling the painting, but until she studies the contracts there's no way to know how binding the sale is. It doesn't look good and we can't take a chance on having the painting tested—my father's painting, that is. If the procedure were sophisticated enough, it might prove that the painting's not sixteenth century.''

''Harriet's aware that a forgery's hanging in her gallery?''

''An emulation, Adam.''

''And are there any other—emulations in the Merrick Gallery?''

She gave him a long, cool look. ''I'm trying not to be annoyed. All of Harriet's paintings are authentic, as is her half of the Titian.''

''Why didn't she replace it herself?''

''Because,'' Kirby began and checked her watch. Time was slipping away from her. ''Not only would it have been difficult for her to disappear from the party early as we did, but it would've been awkward alto-gether. The night watchman could report to Stuart that she came to the gallery in the middle of the night carrying a package. He might put two and two to-gether. Yes, even he might add it up."

"So what'll the night watchman have to say about Kirby Fairchild coming into the gallery in the middle of the night?"

"He won't see us." Her smile was quick and very, very smug.

"Us?"

"Since you're here." She smiled at him again, and meant it. "I've told you everything, and being a gentleman you'll help me make the switch. We'll have to work quickly. If we're caught, we'll just brazen it out. You won't have to do anything, I'll handle it."

"You'll handle it." He nodded at the drifting clouds. "We can all sleep easy now. One condition." He stopped her before she could speak. "When we're done, if we're not in jail or hospitalized, I want to know it all. If we are in jail, I'll murder you as slowly as possible."

"That's two conditions," she muttered. "But all right."

They watched each other a moment, one wonder-ing how much would have to be divulged, one won-dering how much could be learned. Both found the deceit unpleasant.

"Let's get it done." Adam gestured for her to go first.

Kirby walked across the grass and went directly to the main door. From the deep pocket of her cloak, she drew out keys.

"These two switch off the main alarm," she explained as she turned keys in a series of locks. "And these unbolt the door." She smiled at the faint click of tumblers. Turning, she studied Adam, standing behind her in his elegant dinner suit. "I'm so glad we dressed for it."

"Seems right to dress formally when you're breaking into a distinguished institution."

"True." Kirby dropped the keys back in her pocket. "And we do make a rather stunning couple. The Titian hangs in the west room on the second floor. The watchman has a little room in the back, here on the main floor. I assume he drinks black coffee laced with rum and reads pornographic magazines. I would. He's supposed to make rounds hourly, though there's no way to be certain he's diligent."

"And what time does he make them, if he does?"

"On the hour—which give us twenty minutes." She glanced at her watch and shrugged. "That's adequate, though if you hadn't pressed me for details we'd've had more time. Don't scowl," she added. She pressed her finger to her lips and slipped through the door.

From out of the depths of her pocket came a flashlight. They followed the narrow beam over the carpet. Together they moved up the staircase.

Obviously she knew the gallery well. Without hesitation, she moved through the dark, turning on the second floor and marching down the corridor without breaking rhythm. Her cape swirled out as she pivoted into a room. In silence she played her light over paintings until it stopped on the copy of the Titian that had hung in Adam's room.

"There," Kirby whispered as the light shone on the sunset hair Titian immortalized. The light was too poor for Adam to be certain of the quality, but he promised himself to examine it minutes later.

"It's not possible to tell them apart—not even an expert." She knew what he was thinking. "Harriet's a respected authority, and she couldn't. I'm not sure the tests wouldn't bear it out as authentic. Papa has a way of treating the paints." She moved closer so that her light illuminated the entire painting. "Papa put a red circle on the back of the copy's frame so they could be told apart. I'll take the package now," she told him briskly. "You can get the painting down." She knelt and began to unwrap the painting they'd brought with them. "I'm glad you happened along," she decided. "Your height's going to be an advantage when it comes to taking down and putting up again."

Adam paused with the forgery in his hands. Throttling her would be too noisy at the moment, he decided. But later... "Let's have it then."

In silence they exchanged paintings. Adam replaced his on the wall, while Kirby wrapped the other. After she'd tied the string, she played the light on the wall again. "It's a bit crooked," she decided. "A little to the left."

"Look, I—" Adam broke off at the sound of a faint, tuneless whistle.

"He's early!" Kirby whispered as she gripped the painting. "Who expects efficiency from hired help these days?"

In a quick move Adam had the woman, the painting and himself pressed against the wall by the archway. Finding herself neatly sandwiched, and partially smothered, Kirby held back a desperate urge to giggle. Certain it would annoy Adam, she held her breath and swallowed.

The whistle grew louder.

In her mind's eye, Kirby's pictured the watchman strolling down the corridor, pausing to shine his light here and there as he walked. She hoped for the watchman's peace of mind, and Adam's disposition, the search was cursory.

Adam felt her trembling and held her tighter. Somehow he'd manage to protect her. He forgot that she'd gotten him into the mess in the first place. Now his only thought was to get her out of it.

A beam of light streamed passed the doorway, with the whistle close behind. Kirby shook like a leaf. The light bounced into the room, sweeping over the walls in a curving arch. Adam tensed, knowing discovery was inches away. The light halted, rested a moment, then streaked away over its original route. And there was darkness.

They didn't move, though Kirby wanted to badly with the frame digging into her back. They waited, still and silent, until the whistling receded.

Because her light trembling had become shudder after shudder, Adam drew her away to whisper reassurance. "It's all right. He's gone."

"You were wonderful." She covered her mouth to muffle the laughter. "Ever thought about making breaking and entering a hobby?"

He slid the painting under one arm then took a firm grip on hers. When the time was right, he'd pay her back for this one. "Let's go."

"Okay, since it's probably a bad time to show you around. Pity," she decided. "There are some excellent engravings in the next room, and a really marvelous still life Papa painted."

"Under his own name?"

"Really, Adam." They paused at the hallway to make certain it was clear. "That's tacky."

They didn't speak again until they were hidden by the trees, then Adam turned to her. "I'll take the painting and follow you back. If you go over fifty, I'll murder you."

She stopped when they reached the cars, then threw him off balance with suddenly serious eyes. "I appreciate everything, Adam. I hope you don't think too badly of us. It matters."

He ran a finger down her cheek. "I've yet to decide what I think of you."

Her lips curved up at the corners. "That's all right then. Take your time."

"Get in and drive," he ordered before he could forget what had to be resolved. She had a way of making a man forget a lot of things. Too many things.

The trip back took nearly twice the time as Kirby stayed well below the speed limit. Again she left the Porsche out front, knowing Cards would handle the details. Once inside, she went straight to the parlor.

"Well," she mused as she looked at her father. "He seems comfortable enough, but I think I'll just stretch him out."

Adam leaned against the doorjamb and waited as she settled her father for the night. After loosening his tie and pulling off his shoes, she tossed her cape over him and kissed his balding head. "Papa," she murmured. "You've been outmaneuvered."

"We'll talk upstairs, Kirby. Now."

Straightening, Kirby gave Adam a long, mild look. "Since you ask so nicely." She plucked a decanter of brandy and two glasses from the bar. "We may as well be sociable during the inquisition." She swept by him and up the stairs.

Chapter 8

Kirby switched on the rose-tinted bedside lamp before she poured brandy. After handing Adam a snifter, she kicked off her shoes and sat cross-legged on the bed. She watched as he ripped off the wrapping and examined the painting.

Frowning, he studied the brush strokes, the use of color, the Venetian technique that had been Titian's. Fascinating, he thought. Absolutely fascinating. "This is a copy?"

She had to smile. She warmed the brandy between her hands but didn't drink. "Papa's mark's on the frame."

Adam saw the red circle but didn't find it conclusive. "I'd swear it was authentic."

"So would anyone."

He propped the painting against the wall and turned to her. She looked like an Indian priestess—the nightfall of hair against the virgin white silk. With an enigmatic smile, she continued to sit in the lotus position, the brandy cupped in both hands.

"How many other paintings in your father's collection are copies?"

Slowly she lifted the snifter and sipped. She had to work at not being annoyed by the question, telling herself he was entitled to ask, "All of the paintings in Papa's collection are authentic. Excepting now this Titian." She moved her shoulders carelessly. It hardly mattered at this point.

"When you spoke of his technique in treating paints for age, you didn't give the impression he'd only used it on one painting."

What had given her the idea he wouldn't catch on to a chance remark like that one, she wondered. The fat's in the fire in any case, she reminded herself. And she was tired of trying to dance around it. She swirled her drink and red and amber lights glinted against the glass.

"I trust you," she murmured, surprising them both. "But I don't want to involve you, Adam, in something you'll regret knowing about. I really want you to understand that. Once I tell you, it'll be too late for regrets."

He didn't care for the surge of guilt. Who was deceiving whom now? his conscience demanded of him. And who'll pay the price in the end? "Let me worry about that," he stated, dealing with Kirby now and saving his conscience for later. He swallowed brandy and let the heat ease through him. "How many copies has your father done?"

"Ten—no, eleven," she corrected and ignored his quick oath. "Eleven, not counting the Titian, which falls into a different category."

"A different category," he murmured. Crossing the room, he splashed more brandy into his glass. He was certain to need it. "How is this different?"

"The Titian was a personal agreement between Harriet and Papa. Merely a way to avoid bad feelings."

"And the others?" He sat on a fussily elegant Queen Anne chair. "What sort of arrangements did they entail?"

"Each is individual, naturally." She hesitated as she studied him. If they'd met a month from now, would things have been different? Perhaps. Timing again, she mused and sipped the warming brandy. "To simplify matters, Papa painted them, then sold them to interested parties."

"Sold them?" He stood because he couldn't be still. Wishing it had been possible to stop her before she'd begun, he started to pace the room. "Good God, Kirby. Don't you understand what he's done? What he's doing? It's fraud, plain and simple."

"I wouldn't call it fraud," she countered, giving her brandy a contemplative study. It was, after all, something she'd given a great deal of thought to. "And certainly not plain or simple."

"What then?" If he'd had a choice, he'd have taken her away then and there—left the Titian, the Rembrandt and her crazy father in the ridiculous castle and taken off. Somewhere. Anywhere.

"Fudging," Kirby decided with a half smile.

"Fudging," he repeated in a quiet voice. He'd forgotten she was mad as well. "Fudging. Selling counterfeit paintings for large sums of money to the unsuspecting is fudging? Fixing a parking ticket's fudging." He paced another moment, looking for answers. "Damn it, his work's worth a fortune. Why does he do it?"

"Because he can," she said simply. She spread one hand, palm out. "Papa's a genius, Adam. I don't say that just as his daughter but as a fellow artist. With the genius comes a bit of eccentricity perhaps." Ignoring the sharp sound of derision, she went on. "To Papa, painting's not just a vocation. Art and life are one, interchangeable."

"I'll go along with all that, Kirby, but it doesn't explain why—"

"Let me finish." She had both hands on the snifter again, resting it in her lap. "One thing Papa can't tolerate is greed, in any form. To him greed isn't just the worship of money, but the hoarding of art. You must know his collection's constantly being lent out to museums and art schools. Though he has strong feelings that art belongs in private sectors as well as public institutions, he hates the idea of the wealthy buying up great art for investment purposes."

"Admirable, Kirby. But he's made a business out of selling fradulent paintings."

"Not a business. He's never benefited financially." She set her glass aside and clasped her hands together. "Each prospective buyer of one of Papa's emulations is first researched thoroughly." She waited a beat. "By Harriet."

He nearly sat back down again. "Harriet Merrick's in on all of this?"

"All of this," she said mildly, "has been their joint hobby for the last fifteen years."

"Hobby," he murmured and did sit.

"Harriet has very good connections, you see. She makes certain the buyer is very wealthy and that he or she lives in a remote location. Two years ago, Papa sold an Arabian sheik a fabulous Renoir. It was one of my favorites. Anyway—" she continued, getting up to freshen Adam's drink, then her own "—each buyer would also be known for his or her attachment to money, and/or a complete lack of any sense of community spirit or obligation. Through Harriet, they'd learn of Papa's ownership of a rare, officially undiscovered artwork."

Taking her own snifter, she returned to her position on the bed while Adam remained silent. "At the first contact, Papa is always uncooperative without being completely dismissive. Gradually he allows himself to be worn down until the deal's made. The price, naturally, is exorbitant, otherwise the art fanciers would be insulted." She took a small sip and enjoyed the warm flow of the brandy. "He deals only in cash so there's no record. Then the paintings float off to the Himalayas or Siberia or somewhere to be kept in seclusion. Papa then donates the money anonymously to charity."

Taking a deep breath at the end of her speech, Kirby rewarded herself with more brandy.

"You're telling me that he goes through all that, all the work, all the intrigue, for nothing?"

"I certainly am not." Kirby shook her head and leaned forward. "He gets a great deal. He gets satisfaction, Adam. What else is necessary after all?"

He struggled to remember the code of right and wrong. "Kirby, he's stealing!"

Kirby tilted her head and considered. "Who caught your support and admiration, Adam? The Sheriff of Nottingham or Robin Hood?"

"It's not the same." He dragged a hand through his hair as he tried to convince them both. "Damn it, Kirby, it's not the same."

"There's a newly modernized pediatric wing at the local hospital," she began quietly. "A little town in Appalachia has a new fire engine and modern equipment. Another in the dust bowl has a wonderful new library."

"All right." He rose again to cut her off. "In fifteen years I'm sure there's quite a list. Maybe in some strange way it's commendable, but it's also illegal, Kirby. It has to stop."

"I know." Her simple agreement broke his rhythm. With a half smile Kirby moved her shoulders. "It was fun while it lasted, but I've known for some time it had to stop before something went wrong. Papa has a project in mind for a series of paintings and I've convinced him to begin soon. It should take him about five years and give us a breathing space. But in the meantime, he's done something I don't know how to cope with."

She was about to give him more. Even before she spoke, Adam knew Kirby was going to give him all her trust. He sat in silence, despising himself as she told him everything she knew about the Rembrandt.

"I imagine part of it's revenge on Stuart," she continued while Adam smoked in silence and she again swirled her brandy without drinking. "Somehow Stuart found out about Papa's hobby and threatened exposure the night I broke our engagement. Papa told me not to worry, that Stuart wasn't in a position to make waves. At the time I had no idea about the Rembrandt business."

She was opening up to him, no questions, no hesitation. He was going to probe, God help him, he hadn't a choice. "Do you have any idea where he might've hidden it?"

"No, but I haven't looked." When she looked at him, she wasn't the sultry gypsy or the exotic princess. She was only a daughter concerned about an adored father. "He's a good man, Adam. No one knows that better than I. I know there's a reason for what he's done and for the time being, I have to accept that. I don't expect you to share my loyalty, just my confidence." He didn't speak and she took his silence for agreement. "My main concern now is that Papa's underestimating Stuart's ruthlessness."

"He won't when you tell him about the scene in the library."

"I'm not going to tell him. Because," she continued before Adam could argue, "I have no way of predicting his reaction. You may have noticed, Papa's a very volatile man." Tilting her glass, she met his gaze with a quick change of mood. "I don't want you to worry about all this, Adam. Talk to Papa about it if you like. Have a chat with Harriet, too. Personally, I find it helpful to tuck the whole business away from time to time and let it hibernate. Like a grizzly bear."

"Grizzly bear."

She laughed and rose. "Let me get you some more brandy."

He stopped her with a hand on her wrist. "Have you told me everything?"

With a frown, she brushed at a speck of lint on the bedspread. "Did I mention the Van Gogh?"

"Oh, God." He pressed his fingers to his eyes. Somehow he'd hoped there'd be an end without really believing it. "What Van Gogh?"

Kirby pursed her lips. "Not exactly a Van Gogh."

"Your father?"

"His latest. He's sold it to Victor Alvarez, a coffee baron in South America." She smiled as Adam said nothing and stared straight ahead. "The working conditions on his farm are deplorable. Of course, there's nothing we can do to remedy that, but Papa's already allocated the purchase price for a school somewhere in the area. It's his last for several years, Adam," she added as he sat with his fingers pressed against his eyes. "And really, I think he'll be pleased that you know all about everything. He'd love to show this painting to you. He's particularly pleased with it."

Adam rubbed his hands over his face. It didn't surprise him to hear himself laughing. "I suppose I should be grateful he hasn't decided to do the ceiling in the Sistine chapel."

"Only after he retires," Kirby put in cheerfully. "And that's years off yet."

Not certain whether she was joking or not, he let it pass. "I've got to give all this a little time to settle."

"Fair enough."

He wasn't going back to his room to report to McIntyre, he decided as he set his brandy aside. He wasn't ready for that yet, so soon after Kirby shared it all with him without questions, without limitations. It wasn't possible to think about his job, or remember outside obligations when she looked at him with all her trust. No, he'd find a way, somehow, to justify what he chose to do in the end. Right and wrong weren't so well defined now.

Looking at her he needed to give, to soothe, to show her she'd been right to give him that most precious of gifts—unqualified trust. Perhaps he didn't deserve it, but he needed it. He needed her.

Without a word, he pulled her into his arms and crushed his mouth to hers, no patience, no requests. Before either of them could think, he drew down the zipper at the back of her dress.

She wanted to give to him—anything, everything he wanted. She didn't want to question him but to forget all the reasons why they shouldn't be together. It would be so easy to drown in the flood of feeling that was so new and so unique. And yet, anything real, anything strong was never easy. She'd been taught from an early age that the things that mattered most were the hardest to obtain. Drawing back, she determined to put things back on a level she could deal with.

"You surprise me," she said with a smile she had to work at.

He pulled her back. She wouldn't slip away from him this time. "Good."

"You know, most women expect a seduction, no matter how perfunctory."

The amusement might be in her eyes, but he could feel the thunder of her heart against his. "Most women aren't Kirby Fairchild." If she wanted to play it lightly, he'd do his damnedest to oblige her—as long as the result was the same. "Why don't we call this my next spontaneous act?" he suggested and slipped her dress down her shoulders. "I wouldn't want to bore you with a conventional pursuit."

How could she resist him? The hands light on her skin, the mouth that smiled and tempted? She'd never hesitated about taking what she wanted . . . until now. Perhaps the time had come for the chess game to stop at a stalemate with neither winning all, and neither losing anything.

Slowly she smiled and let her dress whisper almost soundlessly to the floor.

He found her a treasure of cool satin and warm flesh. She was as seductive, as alluring as he'd known she'd be. Once she'd decided to give, there were no restrictions. In a simple gesture she opened her arms to him and they came together.

Soft sighs, low murmurs, skin against skin. Moonlight and the rose tint from the lamp competed then merged as the mattress yielded under their weight. Her mouth was hot and open, her arms strong. As she moved under him, inviting, taunting, he forgot how small she was.

Everything. All. Now. Needs drove them both to take without patience, and yet . . . Somehow beneath the passion, under the heat, was a tenderness neither had expected from the other.

He touched. She trembled. She tasted. He throbbed. They wanted until the air seemed to spark with it.

With each second both of them found more of what they'd needed, but the findings brought more greed. Take, she seemed to say, then give and give and give.

She had no time to float, only to throb. For him. From him. Her body craved—yearn was too soft a word. She required him, something unique for her. And he with a kiss, with a touch of his hand, could raise her up to planes she'd only dreamed existed. Here was the completion, here was the delight she'd hoped for without truly believing in. This was what she'd wanted so desperately in her life but had never found. Here and now. Him. There was and needed to be nothing else.

He edged toward madness. She held him, hard and tight as they swung toward the edge together. Together was all she could think. Together.

Quiet. It was so quiet there might never have been such a thing as sound. Her hair brushed against his cheek. Her hand, balled into a loose fist, lay over his heart. Adam lay in the silence and hurt as he'd never expected to hurt.

How had he let it happen? Control? What had made him think he had control when it came to Kirby? Somehow she'd wrapped herself around him, body and mind, while he'd been pretending he'd known exactly what he'd been doing.

He'd come to do a job, he reminded himself. He still had to do it, no matter what had passed between them. Could he go on with what he'd come to do, and protect her? Was it possible to split himself in two when his road had always been so straight? He wasn't certain of anything now, but the tug-of-war he'd lose whichever way the game ended. He had to think, create the distance he needed to do so. Better for both of them if he started now.

But when he shifted away, she held him tighter. Kirby lifted her head so that moonlight caught in her eyes and mesmerized him. "Don't go," she murmured. "Stay and sleep with me. I don't want it to end yet."

He couldn't resist her now. Perhaps he never would. Saying nothing, Adam drew her close again and closed his eyes. For a little while he could pretend tomorrow would take care of itself.

Sunlight woke her, but Kirby tried to ignore it by piling pillows on top of her head. It didn't work for long. Resigned, she tossed them on the floor and lay quietly, alone.

She hadn't heard Adam leave, nor had she expected him to stay until morning. As it was, she was grateful to have woken alone. Now she could think.

How was it she'd given her complete trust to a man she hardly knew? No answer. Why hadn't she evaded his questions, skirted her way around certain facts as she was well capable of doing? No answer.

It wasn't true. Kirby closed her eyes a moment, knowing she'd been more honest with Adam than she was being with herself. She knew the answer.

She'd given him more than she'd ever given to any man. It had been more than a physical alliance, more than a few hours of pleasure in the night. The essence of self had been shared with him. There was no taking it back now even if both of them would have preferred it.

Unknowingly he'd taken her innocence. Emotional virginity was just as real, just as vital as the physical. And it was just as impossible to reclaim. She, thinking of the night, knew that she had no desire to go back. Now they would both move forward to whatever waited for them.

Rising, she prepared to face the day.

Upstairs in Fairchild's studio, Adam studied the rural landscape. He could feel the agitation and drama. The serene scene leaped with frantic life. Vivid, real, disturbing. Its creator stood beside him, not the Vincent van Gogh who Adam would've sworn had wielded the brush and pallette, but Philip Fairchild.

"It's magnificent," Adam murmured. The compliment was out before he could stop it.

"Thank you, Adam. I'm fond of it." Fairchild spoke as a man who'd long before accepted his own superiority and the responsibility that came with it.

"Mr. Fairchild—"

"Philip," Fairchild interrupted genially. "No reason for formality between us."

Somehow Adam felt even the casual intimacy could complicate an already hopelessly tangled situation. "Philip," he began again, "this is fraud. Your motives might be sterling, but the result remains fraud."

"Absolutely." Fairchild bobbed his head in agreement. "Fraud, misrepresentation, a bald-faced lie without a doubt." He lifted his arms and let them fall. "I'm stripped of defenses."

Like hell, Adam thought grimly. Unless he was very much mistaken, he was about to be treated to the biggest bag of pure, classic bull on record.

"Adam..." Fairchild drew out the name and steepled his hands. "You're an astute man, a rational man. I pride myself on being a good judge of character." As if he were very old and frail, Fairchild lowered himself into a chair. "Then, again, you're imaginative and open-minded—that shows in your work."

Adam reached for the coffee Cards had brought up. "So?"

"Your help with our little problem last night—and your skill in turning my own plot against me—leads me to believe you have the ability to adapt to what some might term the unusual."

"Some might."

"Now." Accepting the cup Adam handed him, Fairchild leaned back. "You tell me Kirby filled you in on everything. Odd, but we'll leave that for now." He'd already drawn his own conclusions there and found them to his liking. He wasn't about to lose on other points. "After what you've been told, can you find one iota of selfishness in my enterprise? Can you see my motive as anything but humanitarian?" On a roll, Fairchild set down his cup and let his hands fall between his bony knees. "Small, sick children, and those less fortunate than ourselves have benefited from my hobby. Not one dollar have I kept, not a dollar, a franc, a sou. Never, never have I asked for credit or honor, that naturally society would be anxious to bestow on me."

"You haven't asked for the jail sentence they'd bestow on you either."

Fairchild tilted his head in acknowledgment but didn't miss a beat. "It's my gift to mankind, Adam.

My payment for the talent awarded to me by a higher power. These hands..." He held them up, narrow, gaunt and oddly beautiful. "These hands hold a skill I'm obliged to pay for in my own way. This I've done." Bowing his head, Fairchild dropped them into his lap. "However, if you must condemn me, I understand."

Fairchild looked, Adam mused, like a stalwart Christian faced by pagan lions: firm in his belief, resigned to his fate. "One day," Adam murmured, "your halo's going to slip and strangle you."

"A possibility." Grinning, he lifted his head again. "But in the meantime, we enjoy what we can. Let's have one of those Danishes, my boy."

Wordlessly, Adam handed him the tray. "Have you considered the repercussions to Kirby if your...hobby is discovered?"

"Ah." Fairchild swallowed pastry. "A straight shot to my Achilles' heel. Naturally both of us know that Kirby can meet any obstacle and find a way over, around or through it." He bit off more Danish, enjoying the tang of raspberry. "Still, merely by being, Kirby demands emotion of one kind or another. You'd agree?"

Adam thought of the night, and what it had changed in him. "Yes."

The brief concise answer was exactly what Fairchild had expected. "I'm taking a hiatus from this business for various reasons, the first of which is Kirby's position."

"And her position as concerns the Merrick Rembrandt?"

"A different kettle of fish." Fairchild dusted his fingers on a napkin and considered another pastry. "I'd like to share the ins and outs of that business with you, Adam, but I'm not free to just yet." He smiled and gazed over Adam's head. "One could say I've involved Kirby figuratively, but until things are resolved, she's a minor player in the game."

"Are you casting as well as directing this performance, Papa?" Kirby walked into the room and picked up the Danish Fairchild had been eyeing. "Did you sleep well, darling?"

"Like a rock, brat," he muttered, remembering the confusion of waking up on the sofa under her cape. He didn't care to be outwitted, but was a man who acknowledged a quick mind. "I'm told your evening activities went well."

"The deed's done." She glanced at Adam before resting her hands on her father's shoulders. The bond was there, unbreakable. "Maybe I should leave the two of you alone for a while. Adam has a way of digging out information. You might tell him what you won't tell me."

"All in good time." He patted her hands. "I'm devoting the morning to my hawk." Rising, he went to uncover his clay, an obvious dismissal. "You might give Harriet a call and tell her all's well before you two amuse yourselves."

Kirby held our her hand. "Have you any amusements in mind, Adam?"

"As a matter of fact . . ." He went with the impulse and kissed her as her father watched and speculated. "I had a session of oils and canvas in mind. You'll have to change."

"If that's the best you can do. Two hours only," she warned as they walked from the room. "Otherwise my rates go up. I have my own work, you know."

"Three."

"Two and a half." She paused at the second-floor landing.

"You looked like a child this morning," he murmured and touched her cheek. "I couldn't bring myself to wake you." He left his hand there only a moment, then moved away. "I'll meet you upstairs."

Kirby went to her room and tossed the red dress on the bed. While she undressed with one hand, she dialed the phone with the other.

"Harriet, it's Kirby to set your mind at rest."

"Clever child. Was there any trouble?"

"No." She wiggled out of her jeans. "We managed."

"We? Did Philip go with you?"

"Papa was snoozing on the couch after Adam switched drinks."

"Oh, dear." Amused, Harriet settled back. "Was he very angry?"

"Papa or Adam?" Kirby countered then shrugged. "No matter, in the end they were both very reasonable. Adam was a great help."

"The test isn't for a half hour. Give me the details."

Struggling in and out of clothes, Kirby told her everything.

"Marvelous!" Pleased with the drama, Harriet beamed at the phone. "I wish I'd done it. I'll have to get to know your Adam better and find some spectacular way of showing him my gratitude. Do you think he'd like the crocodile teeth?''

"Nothing would please him more."

"Kirby, you know how grateful I am to you." Harriet's voice was abruptly serious and maternal. "The situation's awkward to say the least."

"The contract's binding?"

"Yes." She let out a sigh at the thought of losing the Titian. "My fault. I should've explained to Stuart that the painting wasn't to be sold. Philip must be furious with me."

"You can handle him. You always do."

"Yes, yes. Lord knows what I'd do without you, though. Poor Melly just can't understand me as you do."

"She's just made differently." Kirby stared down at the floor and tried not to think about the Rembrandt and the guilt it brought her. "Come to dinner tonight, Harriet, you and Melanie."

"Oh, I'd love to, darling, but I've a meeting. Tomorrow?"

"Fine. Shall I call Melly or will you speak with her?"

"I'll see her this afternoon. Take care and do thank Adam for me. Damn shame I'm too old to give him anything but crocodile teeth."

With a laugh, Kirby hung up.

The sun swept over her dress, shooting it with flames or darkening it to blood. It glinted from the rings at her ears, the bracelets on her arms. Knowing the light was as perfect as it would ever be, Adam worked feverishly.

He was an artist of subtle details, one who used light and shadow for mood. In his portraits he strove for an inner reality, the truth beneath the surface of the model. In Kirby he saw the essence of woman—power and frailty and that elusive, mystical quality of sex. Aloof, alluring. She was both. Now, more than ever, he understood it.

Hours passed without him giving them a thought. His model, however, had a different frame of mind.

"Adam, if you'll consult your watch, you'll see I've given you more than the allotted time already."

He ignored her and continued to paint.

"I can't stand here another moment." She let her arms drop from their posed position then wiggled them from the shoulders down. "As it is, I'll probably never pole vault again."

"I can work on the background awhile," he muttered. "I need another three hours in the morning. The light's best then."

Kirby bit off a retort. Rudeness was something to be expected when an artist was taken over by his art. Stretching her muscles, she went to look over his shoulder.

"You've a good hand with light," she decided as she studied the emerging painting. "It's very flattering, certainly, rather fiery and defiant with the color's you've chosen." She looked carefully at the vague lines of her face, the tints and hues he was using to create her on canvas. "Still, there's a fragility here I don't quite understand."

"Maybe I know you better than you know yourself." He never looked at her, but continued to paint.

In not looking, he didn't see the stunned expression or the gradual acceptance.

Linking her hands together, Kirby wandered away. She'd have to do it quickly, she decided. It needed to be done, to be said. "Adam..."

An inarticulate mutter. His back remained to her.

Kirby took a deep breath. "I love you."

"Umm-hmm."

Some women might've been crushed. Others would've been furious. Kirby laughed and tossed back her hair. Life was never what you expected. "Adam, I'd like just a moment of your attention." Though she continued to smile, her knuckles turned white. "I'm in love with you."

It got through on the second try. His brush, tipped in coral, stopped in midair. Very slowly, he set it down and turned. She was looking at him, the half smile on her face, her hands linked together so tightly they hurt. She hadn't expected a response, nor would she demand one.

"I don't tell you that to put pressure on you, or to embarrass you." Nerves showed only briefly as she moistened her lips. "It's just that I think you have a right to know." Her words began to spill out quickly. "We haven't known each other for long, I know, but I suppose it just happens this way sometimes. I couldn't do anything about it. I don't expect anything from you, permanently or temporarily." When he still didn't speak, she felt a jolt of panic she didn't know how to deal with. Had she ruined it? Now the smile didn't reach her eyes. "I've got to change," she said lightly. "You've made me miss lunch as it is."

She was nearly to the door before he stopped her. As he took her shoulders, he felt her tense. And as he felt it, he understood she'd given him everything that was in her heart. Something he knew instinctively had never been given to any other man.

"Kirby, you're the most exceptional woman I've ever known."

"Yes, someone's always pointing that out." She had to get through the door and quickly. "Are you coming down, or shall I have a tray sent up?"

He lowered his head to the top of hers and wondered how things had happened so quickly, so finally. "How many people could make such a simple and unselfish declaration of love then walk away without asking for anything? From the beginning you haven't done one thing I'd've expected." He brushed his lips over her hair, lightly, so that she hardly felt it. "Don't I get a chance to say anything?"

"It's not necessary."

"Yes, it is." Turning her, he framed her face with his hands. "And I'd rather have my hands on you when I tell you I love you."

She stood very straight and spoke very calmly. "Don't feel sorry for me, Adam. I couldn't bear it."

He started to say all the sweet, romantic things a woman wanted to hear when love was declared. All the traditional, normal words a man offered when he offered himself. They weren't for Kirby. Instead he lifted a brow. "If you hadn't counted on being loved back, you'll have to adjust."

She waited a moment because she had to be certain. She'd take the risk, take any risk if she were certain. As she looked into his eyes, she began to smile.

The tension in her shoulders vanished. "You've brought it on yourself."

"Yeah. I guess I have to live with it."

The smile faded as she pressed against him. "Oh, God, Adam, I need you. You've no idea how much."

He held her just as tightly, just as desperately. "Yes, I do."

Chapter 9

To love and to be loved in return. It was bewildering to Kirby, frightening, exhilarating. She wanted time to experience it, absorb it. Understanding it didn't matter, not now in the first rush of emotion. She only knew that although she'd always been happy in her life, she was being offered more. She was being offered laughter at midnight, soft words at dawn, a hand to hold and a life to share. The price would be a portion of her independence and the loyalty that had belonged only to her father.

To Kirby love meant sharing, and sharing had no restrictions. Whatever she had, whatever she felt, belonged to Adam as much as to herself. Whatever happened between them now, she'd never be able to change that. No longer able to work, she went down from her studio to find him.

The house was quiet in the early evening lull with the staff downstairs making the dinner preparations and gossiping. Kirby had always liked this time of day—after a long productive session in her studio, before the evening meal. These were the hours to sit in front of a roaring fire, or walk along the cliffs. Now there was someone she needed to share those hours with. Stopping in front of Adam's door, she raised a hand to knock.

The murmur of voices stopped her. If Adam had her father in another discussion, he might learn something more about the Rembrandt that would put her mind at ease. While she hesitated, the thumping of the front door knocker vibrated throughout the house. With a shrug, she turned away to answer.

Inside his room, Adam shifted the transmitter to his other hand. "This is the first chance I've had to call in. Besides, there's nothing new."

"You're supposed to check in every night." Annoyed, McIntyre barked into the receiver. "Damn it, Adam, I was beginning to think something had happened to you."

"If you knew these people, you'd realize how ridiculous that is."

"They don't suspect anything?"

"No." Adam swore at the existence of this job.

"Tell me about Mrs. Merrick and Hiller."

"Harriet's charming and flamboyant." He wouldn't say harmless. Though he thought of what he and Kirby had done the night before, he left it alone. Adam had already rationalized the entire business as having nothing to do with his job. Not specifically. That was enough to justify his keeping it from Mc-

Intyre. Instead Adam would tell him what Adam felt applied and nothing more. "Hiller's very smooth and a complete phony. I walked in on him and Kirby in time to keep him from shoving her around."

"What was his reason?"

"The Rembrandt. He doesn't believe her father's keeping her in the dark about it. He's the kind of man who thinks you can always get what you want by knocking the other person around—if they're smaller."

"Sounds like a gem." But he'd heard the change in tone. If Adam was getting involved with the Fairchild woman... No. McIntyre let it go. That they didn't need. "I've got a line on Victor Alvarez."

"Drop it." Adam kept his voice casual knowing full well just how perceptive Mac could be. "It's a wild-goose chase. I've already dug it up and it doesn't have anything to do with the Rembrandt."

"You know best."

"Yeah." McIntyre, he knew, would never understand Fairchild's hobby. "Since we agree about that, I've got a stipulation."

"Stipulation?"

"When I find the Rembrandt, I handle the rest my own way."

"What do you mean your own way? Listen, Adam—"

"My way," Adam cut him off. "Or you find someone else. I'll get it back for you, Mac, but after I do, the Fairchilds are kept out of it."

"Kept out?" McIntyre exploded so that the receiver crackled with static. "How the hell do you expect me to keep them out?"

"That's your problem. Just do it."

"The place is full of crazies," McIntyre muttered. "Must be contagious."

"Yeah. I'll get back to you." With a grin, Adam switched off the transmitter.

Downstairs, Kirby opened the door and looked into the myopic, dark-framed eyes of Rick Potts. Knowing his hand would be damp with nerves, she held hers out. "Hello, Rick. Papa told me you were coming to visit."

"Kirby." He swallowed and squeezed her hand. Just the sight of her played havoc with his glands. "You look mar—marvelous." He thrust drooping carnations into her face.

"Thank you." Kirby took the flowers Rick had partially strangled and smiled. "Come, let me fix you a drink. You've had a long drive, haven't you? Cards, see to Mr. Potts's luggage please," she continued without giving Rick a chance to speak. He'd need a little time, she knew, to draw words together. "Papa should be down soon." She found a club soda and poured it over ice. "He's been giving a lot of time to his new project; I'm sure he'll want to discuss it with you." After handing him his drink, she gestured to a chair. "So, how've you been?"

He drank first, to separate his tongue from the roof of his mouth. "Fine. That is, I had a bit of a cold last week, but I'm much better now. I'd never come to see you if I had any germs."

She turned in time to hide a grin and poured herself a glass of Perrier. "That's very considerate of you, Rick."

"Have you—have you been working?"

"Yes, I've nearly done enough for my spring showing."

"It'll be wonderful," he told her with blind loyalty. Though he recognized the quality of her work, the more powerful pieces intimidated him. "You'll be staying in New York?"

"Yes." She walked over to sit beside him. "For a week."

"Then maybe—that is, I'd love to, if you had the time, of course, I'd like to take you to dinner." He gulped down club soda. "If you had an evening free."

"That's very sweet of you."

Astonished, he gaped, pupils dilating. From the doorway, Adam watched the puppylike adulation of the lanky, somewhat untidy man. In another ten seconds, Adam estimated, Kirby would have him at her feet whether she wanted him there or not.

Kirby glanced up, and her expression changed so subtly Adam wouldn't have noticed if he hadn't been so completely tuned into her. "Adam." If there'd been relief in her eyes, her voice was casual. "I was hoping you'd come down. Rick, this is Adam Haines. Adam, I think Papa mentioned Rick Potts to you the other day."

The message came across loud and clear. Be kind. With an easy smile, Adam accepted the damp handshake. "Yes, Philip said you were coming for a few days. Kirby tells me you work in watercolors."

"She did?" Nearly undone by the fact that Kirby would speak of him at all, Rick simply stood there a moment.

"We'll have to have a long discussion after dinner." Rising, Kirby began to lead Rick gently toward the door. "I'm sure you'd like to rest a bit after your drive. You can find the way to your room, can't you?"

"Yes, yes, of course."

Kirby watched him wander down the hall before she turned back. She walked back to Adam and wrapped her arms around him. "I hate to repeat myself, but I love you."

He framed her face with his hands and kissed her softly, lightly, with the promise of more. "Repeat yourself as often as you like." He stared down at her, suddenly and completely aroused by no more than her smile. He pressed his mouth into her palm with a re-straint that left her weak. "You take my breath away," he murmured. "It's no wonder you turn Rick Potts to jelly."

"I'd rather turn you to jelly."

She did. It wasn't an easy thing to admit. With a half smile, Adam drew her away. "Are you really going to tell him I'm a jealous lover with a stiletto?"

"It's for his own good." Kirby picked up her glass of Perrier. "He's always so embarrassed after he loses control. Did you learn any more from Papa?"

"No." Puzzled, he frowned. "Why?"

"I was coming to see you right before Rick arrived. I heard you talking."

She slipped a hand into his and he fought to keep the tension from being noticeable. "I don't want to press things now." That much was the truth, he thought fiercely. That much wasn't a lie.

"No, you're probably right about that. Papa tends to get obstinate easily. Let's sit in front of the fire for a little while," she said as she drew him over to it. "And do nothing."

He sat beside her, holding her close, and wished things were as simple as they seemed.

Hours went by before they sat in the parlor again, but they were no longer alone. After an enormous meal, Fairchild and Rick settled down with them to continue the ongoing discussion of art and technique. Assisted by two glasses of wine and a half a glass of brandy, Rick began to heap praise on Kirby's work. Adam recognized the warning signals of battle— Fairchild's pink ears and Kirby's guileless eyes.

"Thank you, Rick." With a smile, Kirby lifted her brandy. "I'm sure you'd like to see Papa's latest work. It's an attempt in clay. A bird or something, isn't it, Papa?"

"A bird? A bird?" In a quick circle, he danced around the table. "It's a hawk, you horrid girl. A bird of prey, a creature of cunning."

A veteran, Rick tried to soothe. "I'd love to see it, Mr. Fairchild."

"And so you will." In one dramatic gulp, Fairchild finished off his drink. "I intend to donate it to the Metropolitan."

Whether Kirby's snort was involuntary or contrived, it produced results.

"Do you mock your father?" Fairchild demanded. "Have you no faith in these hands?" He held them out, fingers spread. "The same hands that held you fresh from your mother's womb?"

"Your hands are the eighth wonder of the world," Kirby told him. However..." She set down her glass, sat back and crossed her legs. Meticulously she brought her fingers together and looked over them.

"From my observations, you have difficulty with your structure. Perhaps with a few years of practice, you'll develop the knack of construction."

"Structure?" he sputtered. "Construction?" His eyes narrowed, his jaw clenched. "Cards!" Kirby sent him an easy smile and picked up her glass again. "Cards!"

"Yes, Mr. Fairchild."

"Cards," Fairchild repeated, glaring at the dignified butler who stood waiting in the doorway.

"Yes, Mr. Fairchild."

"Cards!" He bellowed and pranced.

"I believe Papa wants a deck of cards—Cards," Kirby explained. "Playing cards."

"Yes, miss." With a slight bow, Cards went to get some.

"What's the matter with that man?" Fairchild muttered. In hurried motions, he began to clear off a small table. Exquisite Wedgwood and delicate Venetian glass were dumped unceremoniously on the floor. "You'd think I didn't make myself clear."

"It's so hard to get good help these days," Adam said into his glass.

"Your cards, Mr. Fairchild." The butler placed two sealed decks on the table before gliding from the room.

"Now I'll show you about construction." Fairchild pulled up a chair and wrapped his skinny legs around its legs. Breaking the seal on the first deck, he poured the cards on the table. With meticulous care, he leaned one card against another and formed an arch. "A steady hand and a discerning eye," Fairchild mumbled as he began slowly, and with total intensity, to build a house of cards.

"That should keep him out of trouble for a while," Kirby declared. Sending Adam a wink, she turned to Rick and drew him into a discussion on mutual friends.

An hour drifted by over brandy and quiet conversation. Occasionally there was a mutter or a grumble from the architect in the corner. The fire crackled. When Montique entered and jumped into Adam's lap, Rick paled and sprang up.

"You shouldn't do that. She'll be here any second." He set down his glass with a clatter. "Kirby, I think I'll go up. I want to start work early."

"Of course." She watched his retreat before turning to Adam. "He's terrified of Isabelle. Montique got into his room when he was sleeping and curled on his pillow. Isabelle woke Rick with some rather rude comments while she stood on his chest. I'd better go up and make sure everything's in order." She rose, then bent over and kissed him lightly.

"That's not enough."

"No?" The slow smile curved her lips. "Perhaps we'll fix that later. Come on, Montique, let's go find your wretched keeper."

"Kirby..." Adam waited until both she and the puppy were at the doorway. "Just how much rent does Isabelle pay?"

"Ten mice a month," she told him soberly. "But I'm going to raise it to fifteen in November. Maybe she'll be out by Christmas." Pleased with the thought, she led Montique away.

"A fascinating creature, my Kirby," Fairchild commented.

Adam crossed the room and stared down at the huge, erratic card structure Fairchild continued to construct. "Fascinating."

"She's a woman with much below the surface. Kirby can be cruel when she feels justified. I've seen her squash a six-foot man like a bug." He held a card between the index fingers of both hands, then slowly lowered it into place. "You'll notice, however, that her attitude toward Rick is invariably kind."

Though Fairchild continued to give his full attention to his cards, Adam knew it was more than idle conversation. "Obviously she doesn't want to hurt him."

"Exactly." Fairchild began to patiently build another wing. Unless Adam was very much mistaken, the cards were slowly taking on the lines of the house they were in. "She'll take great care not to because she knows his devotion to her is sincere. Kirby's a strong, independent woman. Where her heart's involved, however, she's a marshmallow. There are a handful of people on this earth she'd sacrifice anything she could for. Rick's one of them—Melanie and Harriet are others. And myself." He held a card on the tops of his fingers as if weighing it. "Yes, myself," he repeated softly. "Because of this, the circumstances of the Rembrandt are very difficult for her. She's torn between separate loyalties. Her father, and the woman who's been her mother most of her life."

"You do nothing to change it," Adam accused. Irrationally he wanted to sweep the cards aside, flatten the meticulously formed construction. He pushed his hands into his pockets where they balled into fists. Just how much could he berate Fairchild when he was deceiving Kirby in nearly the same way? "Why don't you give her some explanation. Something she could understand?"

"Ignorance is bliss," Fairchild stated calmly. "In this case, the less Kirby knows, the simpler things are for her."

"You've a hell of a nerve, Philip."

"Yes, yes, that's quite true." He balanced more cards then went back to the subject foremost in his mind. "There've been dozens of men in Kirby's life. She could choose and discard them as other women do clothing. Yet, in her own way, she was always cautious. I think Kirby believed she wasn't capable of loving a man and had decided to settle for much, much less by agreeing to marry Stuart. Nonsense, of course." Fairchild picked up his drink and studied his rambling card house. "Kirby has a great capacity for love. When she loves a man she'll love with unswerving devotion and loyalty. And when she does, she'll be vulnerable. She loves intensely, Adam."

For the first time, he raised his eyes and met Adam's. "When her mother died, she was devastated. I wouldn't want to live to see her go through anything like that again."

What could he say? Less than he wanted to, but still only the truth. "I don't want to hurt Kirby. I'll do everything I can to keep from hurting her."

Fairchild studied him a moment with the pale blue eyes that saw deep and saw much. "I believe you, and hope you find a way to avoid it. Still, if you love her, you'll find a way to mend whatever damage is done.

The game's on, Adam, the rules set. They can't be altered now, can they?''

Adam stared down at the round face. "You know why I'm here, don't you?"

With a cackle, Fairchild turned back to his cards. Yes indeed, Adam Haines was sharp, he thought, pleased. Kirby had called it from the beginning. "Let's just say for now that you're here to paint and to...observe. Yes, to observe." He placed another card. "Go up to her now, you've my blessing if you feel the need for it. The game's nearly over, Adam. Soon enough we'll have to pick up the pieces. Love's tenuous when it's new, my boy. If you want to keep her, be as stubborn as she is. That's my advice."

In long, methodical strokes, Kirby pulled the brush through her hair. She'd turned the radio on low so that the hot jazz was hardly more than a pulse beat. At the sound of a knock, she sighed. "Rick, you really must go to bed. You'll hate yourself in the morning."

Adam pushed open the door. He took a long look at the woman in front of the mirror, dressed in wisps of beige silk and ivory lace. Without a word, he closed and latched the door behind him.

"Oh, my." Setting the brush on her dresser, Kirby turned around with a little shudder. "A woman simply isn't safe these days. Have you come to have your way with me—I hope."

Adam crossed to her. Letting his hands slide along the silk, he wrapped his arms around her. "I was just passing through." When she smiled he lowered his mouth to hers. "I love you, Kirby. More than anyone, more than anything." Suddenly his mouth was fierce, his arms tight. "Don't ever forget it."

"I won't." But her words were muffled against his mouth. "Just don't stop reminding me. Now..." She drew away, inches only and slowly began to loosen his tie. "Maybe I should remind you."

He watched his tie slip to the floor just before she began to ease his jacket from his shoulders. "It might be a good idea."

"You've been working hard," she told him as she tossed his jacket in the general direction of a chair. "I think you should be pampered a bit."

"Pampered?"

"Mmm." Nudging him onto the bed she knelt to take off his shoes. Carelessly she let them drop, followed by his socks, before she began to massage his feet. "Pampering's good for you in small doses."

He felt the pleasure spread through him at the touch that could almost be described as motherly. Her hands were soft, with that ridge of callus that proved they weren't idle. They were strong and clever, belonging both to artist and to woman. Slowly she slid them up his legs, then down—teasing, promising, until he wasn't certain whether to lay back and enjoy, or to grab and take. Before he could do either, Kirby stood and began to unbutton his shirt.

"I like everything about you," she murmured as she tugged the shirt from the waistband of his slacks. "Have I mentioned that?"

"No." He let her loosen the cuffs and slip the shirt from him. Taking her time, Kirby ran her hands up his rib cage to his shoulders. "The way you look." Softly she pressed a kiss to his cheek. "The way you feel."

Then the other. "The way you think." Her lips brushed over his chin. "The way you taste." Unhooking his slacks, she drew them off, inch by slow inch. "There's nothing about you I'd change."

She straddled him and began to trace long lingering kisses over his face and neck. "Once when I wondered about falling in love, I decided there simply wasn't a man I'd like well enough to make it possible." Her mouth paused just above his. "I was wrong."

Soft, warm and exquisitely tender, her lips met his. Pampering...the word drifted through his mind as she gave him more than any man could expect and only a few might dream of. The strength of her body and her mind, the delicacy of both. They were his, and he didn't have to ask. They'd be his as long as his arms could hold her and open wide enough to give her room.

Knowing only that she loved, Kirby gave. His body heated beneath hers, lean and hard. Disciplined. Somehow the word excited her. He knew who he was and what he wanted. He'd work for both. And he wouldn't demand that she lose any part of what she was to suit that.

His shoulders were firm. Not so broad they would overwhelm her, but wide enough to offer security when she needed it. She brushed her lips over them. There were muscles in his arms, but subtle, not something he'd flex to show her his superiority, but there to protect if she chose to be protected. She ran her fingers over them. His hands were clever, elegantly masculine. They wouldn't hold her back from the places she had to go, but they would be there, held out when she returned. She pressed her mouth to one, then the other.

No one had ever loved him just like this—patiently, devotedly. He wanted nothing more than to go on feeling those long, slow strokes of her fingers, those moist lingering traces of her lips. He felt each in every pore. A total experience. He could see the glossy black fall of her hair as it tumbled over his skin and hear the murmur of her approval as she touched him.

The house was quiet again, but for the low simmering sound of the music. The quilt was soft under his back. The light was dim and gentle—the best light for lovers. And while he lay, she loved him until he was buried under layer upon layer of pleasure. This he would give back to her.

He could touch the silk, and her flesh, knowing that both were exquisite. He could taste her lips and know that he'd never go hungry as long as she was there. When he heard her sigh, he knew he'd be content with no other sound. The need for him was in her eyes, clouding them, so that he knew he could live with little else as long as he could see her face.

Patience began to fade in each of them. He could feel her body spring to frantic life wherever he touched. He could feel his own strain from the need only she brought to him. Desperate, urgent, exclusive. If he'd had only a day left to live, he'd have spent every moment of it there, with Kirby in his arms.

She smelled of wood smoke and musky flowers, of woman and of sex, ripe and ready. If he'd had the power, he'd have frozen time just then, as she loomed above him in the moonlight, eyes dark with need, skin flashing against silk.

Then he drew the silk up and over her head so that he could see her as he swore no man would ever see her again. Her hair tumbled down, streaking night against her flesh. Naked and eager, she was every primitive fantasy, every midnight dream. Everything.

Her lips were parted as the breath hurried between them. Passion swamped her so that she shuddered and rushed to take what she needed from him—for him. Everything. Everything and more. With a low sound of triumph, Kirby took him inside her and led the way. Fast, furious.

Her body urged her on relentlessly while her mind exploded with images. Such color, such sound. Such frenzy. Arched back, she moved like lightning, hardly aware of how tightly his hands gripped her hips. But she heard him say her name. She felt him fill her.

The first crest swamped her, shocking her system then thrusting her along to more, and more and more. There was nothing she couldn't have and nothing she wouldn't give. Senseless, she let herself go.

With his hands on her, with the taste of her still on his lips, Adam felt his system shudder on the edge of release. For a moment, only a moment, he held back. He could see her above him poised like a goddess, flesh damp and glowing, hair streaming back as she lifted her hands to it in ecstasy. This he would remember always.

The moon was no longer full, but its light was soft and white. They were still on top of the quilt, tangled close as their breathing settled. As she lay over him, Adam thought of everything Fairchild had said. And everything he could and couldn't do about it.

Slowly their systems settled, but he could find none of the answers he needed so badly. What answers would there be based on lies and half truths?

Time. Perhaps time was all he had now. But how much or how little was no longer up to him. With a sigh, he shifted and ran a hand down her back.

Kirby rose on an elbow. Her eyes were no longer clouded but saucy and clear. She smiled, touched a fingertip to her own lips and then to his. "Next time you're in town, cowboy," she drawled as she tossed her hair over her shoulder. "Don't forget to ask for Lulu."

She'd expected him to grin, but he grabbed her hair and held her just as she was. There was no humor in his eyes, but the intensity she'd seen when he held a paintbrush. His muscles had tensed, she could feel it.

"Adam?"

"No, don't." He forced his hand to relax, then stroked her cheek. It wouldn't be spoiled by the wrong word, the wrong move. "I want to remember you just like this. Fresh from loving with moonlight on your hair."

He was afraid, unreasonably, that he'd never see her like that again—with that half smile inches away from his face. He'd never feel the warmth of her flesh spread over his with nothing, nothing to separate them.

The panic came fast and was very real. Unable to stop it, Adam pulled her against him and held her as if he'd never let her go.

Chapter 10

After thirty minutes of posing, Kirby ordered herself not to be impatient. She'd agreed to give Adam two hours and a bargain was a bargain. She didn't want to think about the time she had left to stand idle, so instead tried to concentrate on her plans for sculpting once her obligation was over. Her *Anger* was nearly finished.

But the sun seemed too warm and too bright. Every so often her mind would go oddly blank until she pulled herself back just to remember where she was.

"Kirby." Adam called her name for the third time and watched as she blinked and focused on him. "Could you wait until the session's over before you take a nap?"

"Sorry." With an effort she cleared her head and smiled at him. "I was thinking of something else."

"Don't think at all if it puts you to sleep," he muttered and slashed scarlet across the canvas. It was right, so right. Nothing he'd ever done had been as right as this painting. The need to finish it was becoming obsessive. "Tilt your head to the right again. You keep breaking the pose."

"Slave driver." But she obeyed and tried to concentrate.

"Cracking the whip's the only way to work with you." With care, he began to perfect the folds in the skirt of her dress. He wanted them soft, flowing, but clearly defined. "You'd better get used to posing for me. I've already several other studies in mind that I'll start after we're married."

Giddiness washed over her. She felt it in waves—physical, emotional—she couldn't tell one from the other. Without thinking, she dropped her arms.

"Damn it, Kirby." He started to swear at her again when he saw how wide and dark her eyes were. "What is it?"

"I hadn't thought . . . I didn't realize that you . . ." Lifting a hand to her spinning head, she walked around the room. The bracelets slid down to her elbow with a musical jingle. "I need a minute," she murmured. Should she feel as though someone had cut off her air? As if her head was three feet above her shoulders?

Adam watched her for a moment. She didn't seem quite steady, he realized. And there was an unnaturally high color in her cheeks. Standing, he took her hand and held her still. "Are you ill?"

"No." She shook her head. She was never ill, Kirby reminded herself. Just a bit tired—and perhaps for the first time in her life, completely overwhelmed. She took a deep breath, telling herself she'd be all right in a moment. "I didn't know you wanted to marry me, Adam."

Was that it, he wondered as he ran the back of his hand over her cheek. Shouldn't she have known? And yet, he remembered, yet everything had happened so fast. "I love you." It was simple for him. Love led to marriage and marriage to family. But how could he have forgotten Kirby wasn't an ordinary woman and anything but simple? "You accused me of being conventional," he reminded her and ran his hands down her hair to her shoulders. "Marriage is a very conventional institution." And one she might not be ready for, he thought with a quick twinge of panic. He'd have to give her room if he wanted to keep her. But how much room did she need, and how much could he give?

"I want to spend my life with you." Adam waited until her gaze had lifted to his again. She looked stunned by his words—a woman like her, Adam thought. Beautiful, sensuous, strong. How was it a woman like Kirby would be surprised to be wanted? Perhaps he'd moved too quickly, and too clumsily. "Anyway you chose, Kirby. Maybe I should've chosen a better time, a better place to ask rather than assume."

"It's not that." Shaky, she lifted a hand to his face. It was so solid, so strong. "I don't need that." His face blurred a moment, and, shaking her head, she moved away again until she stood where she'd been posing. "I've had marriage proposals before—and a good many less binding requests." She managed a smile. He wanted her, not just for today, but for the tomorrows as well. He wanted her just as she was. She felt the tears well up, of love, of gratitude, but blinked them back. When wishes came true it was no time for tears. "This is the one I've been waiting for all of my life, I just didn't expect to be so flustered."

Relieved, he started to cross to her. "I'll take that as a good sign. Still, I wouldn't mind a simple yes."

"I hate to do anything simple."

She felt the room lurch and fade, then his hands on her shoulders.

"Kirby— Good God, there's gas leaking!" As he stood holding her up, the strong, sweet odor rushed over him. "Get out! Get some air! It must be the heater." Giving her a shove toward the door, he bent over the antiquated unit.

She stumbled across the room. The door seemed miles away so that when she finally reached it she had only the strength to lean against the heavy wood and catch her breath. The air was cleaner there. Gulping it in, Kirby willed herself to reach for the knob. She tugged but it held firm.

"Damn it, I told you to get out!" He was already choking on the fumes when he reached her. "The gas is pouring out of that thing!"

"I can't open the door!" Furious with herself, Kirby pulled again. Adam pushed her hands away and yanked himself. "Is it jammed?" she murmured, leaning against him. "Cards will see to it."

Locked, he realized. From the outside. "Stay here." After propping her against the door, Adam picked up a chair and smashed it against the window. The glass cracked, but held. Again, he rammed the chair, and again, until with a final heave, the glass shattered. Moving quickly, he went back for Kirby and held her head near the jagged opening.

"Breathe," he ordered.

For the moment she could do nothing else but gulp fresh air into her lungs and cough it out again. "Someone's locked us in, haven't they?"

He'd known it wouldn't take her long once her head had cleared. Just as he knew better than to try to evade. "Yes."

"We could shout for hours." She closed her eyes and concentrated. "No one would hear us, we're too isolated up here." With her legs unsteady, she leaned against the wall. "We'll have to wait until someone comes to look for us."

"Where's the main valve for that heater?"

"Main valve?" She pressed her fingers to her eyes and forced herself to think. "I just turn the thing on when it's cold up here.... Wait. Tanks—there are tanks out in back of the kitchen." She turned back to the broken window again telling herself she couldn't be sick. "One for each tower and for each floor."

Adam glanced at the small old-fashioned heater again. It wouldn't take much longer, even with the broken window. "We're getting out of here."

"How?" If she could just lay down—just for a minute... "The door's locked. I don't think we'd survive a jump into Jamie's zinnias," she added, looking down to where the chair had landed. But he wasn't listening to her. When Kirby turned she saw Adam running his hand over the ornate trim. The panel yawned open. "How'd you find that one?"

He grabbed her by the elbow and pulled her forward. "Let's go."

"I can't." With the last of her strength, Kirby braced her hands against the wall. Fear and nausea doubled at the thought of going into the dark, dank hole in the wall. "I can't go in there."

"Don't be ridiculous."

When he would've pulled her through, Kirby jerked away and backed up. "No, you go. I'll wait for you to come around and open the door."

"Listen to me." Fighting the fumes, he grabbed her shoulders. "I don't know how long it'd take me to find my way through that maze in the dark."

"I'll be patient."

"You could be dead," he countered between his teeth. "That heater's unstable—if there's a short this whole room would go up! You've already taken in too much of the gas."

"I won't go in!" Hysteria bubbled and she didn't have the strength or the wit to combat it. Her voice rose as she stumbled back from him. "I can't go in, don't you understand?"

"I hope you understand this," he muttered and clipped her cleanly on the jaw. Without a sound, she collapsed into his arms. Adam didn't hesitate. He tossed her unceremoniously over his shoulder and plunged into the passageway.

With the panel closed to cut off the flow of gas, the passage was in total darkness. With one arm holding Kirby in place, Adam inched along the wall. He had to reach the stairs, and the first mechanism. Groping, testing each step, he hugged the wall, knowing what would happen to both of them if he rushed and plunged them headlong down the steep, stone stairway.

He heard the skitter of rodents and brushed spiderwebs out of his face. Perhaps it was best that Kirby was unconscious, he decided. He'd get her through a lot easier carrying her than he would dragging her.

Five minutes, then ten, then at last his foot met empty space.

Cautiously, he shifted Kirby on his shoulder, pressed the other to the wall, and started down. The steps were stone and treacherous enough with a light. In the dark, with no rail for balance, they were deadly. Fighting the need to rush, Adam checked himself on each step before going on to the next. When he reached bottom, he went no faster, but began to trace his hand along the wall, feeling for a switch.

The first one stuck. He had to concentrate just to breathe. Kirby swayed on his shoulder as he maneuvered the sharp turn in the passage. Swearing, Adam moved forward blindly until his fingers brushed over a second lever. The panel groaned open just enough for him to squeeze himself and his burden through. Blinking at the sunlight, he dashed around dust-covered furniture and out into the hall.

When he reached the second floor and passed Cards he didn't break stride. "Turn off the gas to Kirby's studio from the main valve," he ordered, coughing as he moved by. "And keep everyone away from there."

"Yes, Mr. Haines." Cards continued to walk toward the main stairway carrying his pile of fresh linens.

When Adam reached her room, he lay Kirby on the bed then opened the windows. He stood there a moment, just breathing, letting the air rush over his face and soothe his eyes. His stomach heaved. Forcing himself to take slow, measured breaths, he leaned out. When the nausea passed, he went back to her.

The high color had faded. Now she was as pale as the quilt. She didn't move. Hadn't moved, he remembered, since he'd hit her. With a tremor, he pressed his fingers to her throat and felt a slow, steady pulse. Quickly he went into the bathroom and soaked a cloth with cold water. As he ran it over her face, he said her name.

She coughed first, violently. Nothing could've relieved him more. When her eyes opened, she stared at him dully.

"You're in your room," he told her. "You're all right now."

"You hit me."

He grinned because there was indignation in her voice. "I thought you'd take a punch better with a chin like that. I barely tapped you."

"So you say." Gingerly she sat up and touched her chin. Her head whirled once, but she closed her eyes and waited for it to pass. "I suppose I had it coming. Sorry I got neurotic on you."

He let his forehead rest against hers. "You scared the hell out of me. I guess you're the only woman who's received a marriage proposal and a right jab within minutes of each other."

"I hate to do the ordinary." Because she needed another minute, she lay back against the pillows. "Have you turned off the gas?"

"Cards is seeing to it."

"Of course." She said this calmly enough, then began to pluck at the quilt with her fingers. "As far as I know, no one's tried to kill me before."

It made it easier, he thought, that she understood and accepted that straight off. With a nod, he touched a hand to her cheek. "First we call a doctor. Then we call the police."

"I don't need a doctor. I'm just a little queasy now, it'll pass." She took both his hands and held them firmly. "And we can't call the police."

He saw something in her eyes that nearly snapped his temper. Stubbornness. "It's the usual procedure after attempted murder, Kirby."

She didn't wince. "They'll ask annoying questions and skulk all over the house. It's in all the movies."

"This isn't a game." His hands tightened on hers. "You could've been killed—would've been if you'd been in there alone. I'm not giving him another shot at you."

"You think it was Stuart." She let out a long breath. Be objective, she told herself. Then you can make Adam be objective. "Yes, I suppose it was, though I wouldn't have thought him ingenious enough. There's no one else who'd want to hurt me. Still, we can't prove a thing."

"That has yet to be seen." His eyes flashed a moment as he thought of the satisfaction he'd get from beating a confession out of Hiller. She saw it. She understood it.

"You're more primitive than I'd imagined." Touched, she traced her finger down his jaw. "I didn't know how nice it would be to have someone want to vanquish dragons for me. Who needs a bunch of silly police when I have you?''

"Don't try to outmaneuver me."

"I'm not." The smile left her eyes and her lips. "We're not in the position to call the police. I couldn't answer the questions they'd ask, don't you see? Papa has to resolve the business of the Rembrandt, Adam. If everything came out now, he'd be hopelessly compromised. He might go to prison. Not for anything," she said softly. "Not for anything would I risk that."

"He won't," Adam said shortly. No matter what strings he'd have to pull, what dance he'd have to perform, he'd see to it that Fairchild stayed clear. "Kirby, do you think your father would continue with whatever he's plotting once he knew of this?"

"I couldn't predict his reaction." Weary, she let out a long breath and tried to make him understand. "He might destroy the Rembrandt in a blind rage. He could go after Stuart single-handed. He's capable of it. What good would any of that do, Adam?" The queasiness was passing, but it had left her weak. Though she didn't know it, the vulnerability was her best weapon. "We have to let it lie for a while longer."

"What do you mean, let it lie?"

"I'll speak to Papa—tell him what happened in my own way, so that he doesn't overreact. Harriet and Melanie are coming to dinner tonight. It has to wait until tomorrow."

"How can he sit down and have dinner with Harriet when he has stolen something from her?" Adam demanded. "How can he do something like this to a friend?"

Pain shot into her eyes. Deliberately she lowered them, but he'd already seen it. "I don't know."

"I'm sorry."

She shook her head. "No, you have no reason to be. You've been wonderful through all of this."

"No, I haven't." He pressed the heels of his hands to his eyes.

"Let me be the judge of that. And give me one more day." She touched his wrists and waited until he lowered his hands. "Just one more day, then I'll talk to Papa. Maybe we'll get everything straightened out."

"That much, Kirby. No more." He had some thinking of his own to do. Perhaps one more night would give him some answers. "Tomorrow you tell Philip everything, no glossing over the details. If he doesn't agree to resolve the Rembrandt business then, I'm taking over."

She hesitated a minute. She'd said she trusted him. It was true. "All right."

"And I'll deal with Hiller."

"You're not going to fight with him."

Amused, he lifted a brow. "No?"

"Adam, I won't have you bruised and bloodied. That's it."

"Your confidence in me is overwhelming."

With a laugh, she sat up again and threw her arms around him. "My hero. He'd never lay a hand on you."

"I beg your pardon, Miss Fairchild."

"Yes, Cards." Shifting her head, Kirby acknowledged the butler in the doorway.

"It seems a chair has somehow found its way through your studio window. Unfortunately it landed in Jamie's bed of zinnias."

"Yes, I know. I suppose he's quite annoyed."

"Indeed, miss."

"I'll apologize, Cards. Perhaps a new lawn mower... You'll see to having the window repaired?"

"Yes, miss."

"And have that heater replaced by something from the twentieth century," Adam added. He watched as Cards glanced at him then back at Kirby.

"As soon as possible, please, Cards."

With a nod, the butler backed out of the doorway.

"He takes his orders from you, doesn't he?" Adam commented as the quiet footsteps receded. "I've seen the subtle nods and looks between the two of you."

She brushed a smudge of dirt on the shoulder of his shirt. "I've no idea what you mean."

"A century ago, Cards would've been known as the queen's man." When she laughed at the term, he eased her back on the pillows. "Rest," he ordered.

"Adam, I'm fine."

"Want me to get tough again?" Before he could answer, he covered her mouth with his, lingering. "Turn the batteries down awhile," he murmured. "I might have to call the doctor after all."

"Blackmail." She brought his mouth back to hers again. "But maybe if you rested with me..."

"Rest isn't what would happen then." He drew away as she grumbled a protest.

"A half hour."

"Fine. I'll be back."

She smiled and let her eyes close. "I'll be waiting."

It was too soon for stars, too late for sunbeams. From a window in the parlor, Adam watched the sunset hold off twilight just a few moments longer.

After reporting the attempt on Kirby's life to McIntyre, he'd found himself suddenly weary. Half lies, half truths. It had to end. It would end, he decided, tomorrow. Fairchild would have to see reason and Kirby would be told everything. The hell with McIntyre, the job and anything else. She deserved honesty along with everything else he wanted to give her. Everything else, he realized, would mean nothing to Kirby without it.

The sun lowered further and the horizon exploded with rose-gold light. He thought of the Titian woman. She'd understand, he told himself. She had to understand. He'd make her understand. Thinking to check on her again, Adam turned from the window.

When he reached her room, he heard the sound of running water. The simple, natural sound of her humming along with her bath dissolved his tension. He thought about joining her, then remembered how pale and tired she'd looked. Another time, he promised both of them as he shut the door to her room again. Another time he'd have the pleasure of lounging in the big marble tub with her.

"Where's that wretched girl?" Fairchild demanded from behind him. "She's been hiding out all day."

"Having a bath," Adam told him.

"She'd better have a damn good explanation, that's all I have to say." Looking grim, Fairchild reached for the doorknob. Adam blocked the door automatically.

"For what?"

Fairchild glared at him. "My shoes."

Adam looked down at Fairchild's small stockinged feet. "I don't think she has them."

"A man tugs himself into a restraining suit, chokes himself with a ridiculous tie, then has no shoes." Fairchild pulled at the knot around his neck. "Is that justice?"

"No. Have you tried Cards?"

"Cards couldn't get his big British feet in my shoes." Then he frowned and pursed his lips. "Then again, he did have my suit."

"I rest my case."

"The man's a kleptomaniac," Fairchild grumbled as he wandered down the hall. "I'd check my shorts if I were you. No telling what he'll pick up next. Cocktails in a half hour, Adam. Hustle along."

Deciding a quiet drink was an excellent idea after the day they'd put in, Adam went to change. He was adjusting the knot in his own tie when Kirby knocked. She opened it without waiting for his answer, then stood a moment deliberately posed in the doorway— head thrown back, one arm raised high on the jamb, the other at her hip. The slinky jumpsuit clung to every curve, falling in folds from her neck and dispensing with a back altogether. At her ears, emeralds the size of quarters picked up the vivid green shade. Five twisted, gold chains hung past her waist.

"Hello, neighbor." Glittering and gleaming, she crossed to him. Adam put a finger under her chin and studied her face. As an artist she knew how to make use of the colors of a makeup palette. Her cheeks were tinted with a touch of bronze, her lips just a bite darker. "Well?"

"You look better," he decided.

"That's a poor excuse for a compliment."

"How do you feel?"

"I'd feel a lot better if you'd stop examining me as though I had a rare terminal disease and kiss me as you're supposed to." She twisted her arms around his neck and let her lashes lower.

It was them he kissed first, softly, with a tenderness that had her sighing. Then his lips skimmed down, over her cheeks, gently over her jawline.

"Adam..." His name was only a breath on the air as his mouth touched hers. She wanted it all now. Instantly. She wanted the fire and flash, the pleasure and the passion. She wanted that calm, spreading contentment that only he could give to her. "I love you," she murmured. "I love you until there's nothing else but that."

"There is nothing else but that," he said almost fiercely. "We've a lifetime for it." He drew her away so he could bring both of her hands to his lips. "A lifetime, Kirby, and it isn't long enough."

"Then we'll have to start soon." She felt the giddiness again, the light-headedness, but she wouldn't run from it. "Very soon," she added. "But we have to wait at least until after dinner. Harriet and Melanie should be here any minute."

"If I had my choice, I'd stay with you alone in this room and make love until sunrise."

"Don't tempt me to tarnish your reputation." Because she knew she had to, she stepped back and finished adjusting his tie herself. It was a brisk, womanly gesture he found himself enjoying. "Ever since I told Harriet about your help with the Titian, she's decided you're the greatest thing since peanut butter. I wouldn't want to mess that up by making you late for dinner."

"Then we'd better go now. Five more minutes alone with you and we'd be a lot more than late." When she laughed, he linked her arm through his and led her from the room. "By the way, your father's shoes were stolen."

To the casual observer, the group in the parlor would have seemed a handful of elegant, cosmopolitan people. Secure, friendly, casually wealthy. Looking beyond the sparkle and glitter, a more discerning eye might have seen the pallor of Kirby's skin that her careful application of makeup disguised. Someone looking closely might have noticed that her friendly nonsense covered a discomfort that came from battling loyalties.

To someone from the outside, the group might have taken on a different aspect if the canvas were stretched. Rick's stuttering nerves were hardly noticed by those in the parlor. As was Melanie's subtle disdain for him. Both were the expected. Fairchild's wolfish grins and Harriet's jolting laughter covered the rest.

Everyone seemed relaxed, except Adam. The longer it went on, the more he wished he'd insisted that Kirby postpone the dinner party. She looked frail. The more energy she poured out, the more fragile she seemed to him. And touchingly valiant. Her devotion to Harriet hadn't been lip service. Adam could see it, hear it. When she loved, as Fairchild had said, she loved completely. Even the thought of the Rembrandt would be tearing her in two. Tomorrow. By the next day, it would be over.

"Adam." Harriet took his arm as Kirby poured after-dinner drinks. "I'd love to see Kirby's portrait."

"As soon as it's finished you'll have a private viewing." And until the repairs in the tower were complete, he thought, he was keeping all outsiders away.

"I'll have to be content with that, I suppose." She pouted a moment, then forgave him. "Sit beside me," Harriet commanded and spread the flowing vermilion of her skirt on the sofa. "Kirby said I could flirt with you."

Adam noticed that Melanie turned a delicate pink at her mother's flamboyance. Unable to resist, he lifted Harriet's hand to his lips. "Do I need permission to flirt with you?"

"Guard your heart, Harriet," Kirby warned as she set out drinks.

"Mind your own business," Harriet tossed back. "By the way, Adam, I'd like you to have my necklace of crocodile teeth as a token of my appreciation."

"Good heavens, Mother." Melanie sipped at her blackberry brandy. "Why would Adam want that hideous thing?"

"Sentiment," she returned without blinking an eye. "Adam's agreed to let me exhibit Kirby's portrait and I want to repay him."

The old girl's quick, Adam decided as she sent him a guileless smile, and Melanie's been kept completely in the dark about the hobby her mother shares with Fairchild. Studying Melanie's cool beauty, Adam decided her mother knew best. She'd never react as Kirby did. Melanie could have their love and affection, but secrets were kept within the triangle. No, he realized, oddly pleased. It was now a rectangle.

"He doesn't have to wear it," Harriet went on, breaking into his thoughts.

"I should hope not," Melanie put in, rolling her eyes at Kirby.

"It's for good luck." Harriet sent Kirby a glance then squeezed Adam's arm. "But perhaps you have all the luck you need."

"Perhaps my luck's just beginning."

"How quaintly they speak in riddles." Kirby sat on the arm of Melanie's chair. "Why don't we ignore them?"

"Your hawk's coming along nicely, Mr. Fairchild," Rich hazarded.

"Aha!" It was all Fairchild needed. Bursting with good feelings, he treated Rick to an in-depth lecture on the use of calipers.

"Rick's done it now," Kirby whispered to Melanie. "Papa has no mercy on a captive audience."

"I didn't know Uncle Philip was sculpting."

"Don't mention it," Kirby said quickly. "You'll never escape." Pursing her lips, she looked down at Melanie's elegant dark rose dress. The lines flowed fluidly with the flash of a studded buckle at the waist. "Melly, I wonder if you'd have time to design a dress for me."

Surprised, Melanie glanced up. "Oh course, I'd love to. But I've been trying to talk you into it for years and you've always refused to go through the fittings."

Kirby shrugged. A wedding dress was a different matter, she mused. Still, she didn't mention her plans with Adam. Her father would know first. "I usually buy on impulse, whatever appeals at the time."

"From Goodwill to Rive Gauche," Melanie murmured. "So this must be special."

"I'm taking a page from your book," Kirby evaded. "You know I've always admired your talent, I just knew I wouldn't have the patience for all the preliminaries." She laughed. "Do you think you can design a dress that'd make me look demure?"

"Demure?" Harriet cut in, pouncing on the word. "Poor Melanie would have to be a sorceress to pull that off. Even as a child in that sweet little muslin you looked capable of battling a tribe of Comanches. Philip, you must let me borrow that painting of Kirby for the gallery."

"We'll see." His eyes twinkled. "You'll have to soften me up a bit first. I've always had a deep affection for that painting." With a hefty sigh, he leaned back with his drink. "Its value goes below the surface."

"He still begrudges me my sitting fee." Kirby sent her father a sweet smile. "He forgets I never collected for any of the others."

"You never posed for the others," Fairchild reminded her.

"I never signed a release for them, either."

"Melly posed for me out of the goodness of her heart."

"Melly's nicer than I am," Kirby said simply. "I like being selfish."

"Heartless creature," Harriet put in mildly. "It's so selfish of you to teach sculpture in the summer to those handicapped children."

Catching Adam's surprised glance, Kirby shifted uncomfortably. "Harriet, think of my reputation."

"She's sensitive about her good deeds," Harriet told Adam with a squeeze for his knee.

"I simply had nothing else to do." With a shrug, Kirby turned away. "Are you going to Saint Moritz this year, Melly?"

Fraud, Adam thought as he watched her guide the subject away from herself. A beautiful, sensitive fraud. And finding her so, he loved her more.

By the time Harriet and Melanie rose to leave, Kirby was fighting off a raging headache. Too much strain, she knew, but she wouldn't admit it. She could tell herself she needed only a good night's sleep, and nearly believe it.

"Kirby." Harriet swirled her six-foot shawl over her shoulder before she took Kirby's chin in her hand. "You look tired, and a bit pale. I haven't seen you look pale since you were thirteen and had the flu. I remember you swore you'd never be ill again."

"After that disgusting medicine you poured down my throat I couldn't afford to. I'm fine." But she threw her arms around Harriet's neck and held on. "I'm fine, really."

"Mmm." Over her head, Harriet frowned at Fairchild. "You might think about Australia. We'll put some color in your cheeks."

"I will. I love you."

"Go to sleep, child," Harriet murmured.

The moment the door was closed, Adam took Kirby's arm. Ignoring her father and Rick, he began to pull her up the stairs. "You belong in bed."

"Shouldn't you be dragging me by the hair instead of the arm?"

"Some other time when my intentions are less peaceful." He stopped outside her door. "You're going to sleep."

"Tired of me already?"

The words were hardly out of her mouth when his covered it. Holding her close, he let himself go for a moment, releasing the needs, the desires, the love. He could feel her heart thud, her bones melt. "Can't you see how tired I am of you?" He kissed her again with his hands framing her face. "You must see how you bore me."

"Anything I can do?" she murmured, slipping her hands under his jacket.

"Get some rest." He took her by the shoulders. "This is your last opportunity to sleep alone."

"Am I sleeping alone?"

It wasn't easy for him. He wanted to devour her, he wanted to delight her. He wanted, more than anything else, to have a clean slate between them before they made love again. If she hadn't looked so weary, so worn, he'd have told her everything then and there. "This may come as a shock to you," he said lightly. "But you're not Wonder Woman."

"Really?"

"You're going to get a good night's sleep. Tomorrow." He took her hands and the look, the sudden intenseness confused her. "Tomorrow, Kirby, we have to talk."

"About what?"

"Tomorrow," he repeated before he could change his mind. "Rest now." He gave her a nudge inside. "If you're not feeling any better tomorrow you're going to stay in bed and be pampered."

She managed one last wicked grin. "Promise?"

Chapter 11

It was clear after Kirby had tossed in bed and fluffed up her pillow for more than an hour, that she wasn't going to get the rest everyone seemed to want for her. Her body was dragging, but her mind refused to give in to it.

She tried. For twenty minutes she recited dull poetry. Closing her eyes, she counted five hundred and twenty-seven camels. She turned on her bedside radio and found chamber music. She was, after all of it, wide awake.

It wasn't fear. If Stuart had indeed tried to kill her, he'd failed. She had her own wits, and she had Adam. No, it wasn't fear.

The Rembrandt. She couldn't think of anything else after seeing Harriet laughing, after remembering how Harriet had nursed her through the flu and had given her a sweet and totally unnecessary woman to woman talk when she'd been a girl.

Kirby had grieved for her own mother, and though she'd died when Kirby had been a child, the memory remained perfectly clear. Harriet hadn't been a substitute. Harriet had simply been Harriet. Kirby loved her for that alone.

How could she sleep?

Annoyed, Kirby rolled over on her back and stared at the ceiling. Maybe, just maybe she could make use of the insomnia and sort it all out and make some sense out of it.

Her father, she was certain, would do nothing to hurt Harriet without cause. Was revenge on Stuart cause enough? After a moment, she decided it didn't follow.

Harriet had gone to Africa—that was first. It had been nearly two weeks after that when Kirby had broken her engagement with Stuart. Afterward she had told her father of Stuart's blackmail threats and he'd been unconcerned. He's said, Kirby remembered, that Stuart wasn't in any position to make waves.

Then it made sense to assume they'd already begun plans to switch the paintings. Revenge was out.

Then why?

Not for money, Kirby thought. Not for the desire to own the painting himself. That wasn't his way—she knew better than anyone how he felt about greed. But then stealing from a friend wasn't his way either.

If she couldn't find the reason, perhaps she could find the painting itself.

Still staring at the ceiling, she began to go over everything her father had said. So many ambiguous comments, she mused. But then, that was typical of him. In the house—that much was certain. In the house, hidden with appropriate affection and respect. Just how many hundreds of possibilities could she sort through in one night?

She blew out a disgusted breath and rolled over again. With a last thump for her pillow, she closed her eyes. The yawn, she felt, was a hopeful sign. As she snuggled deeper, a tiny memory probed.

She'd think about it tomorrow.... No, now, she thought and rolled over again. She'd think about it now. What was it her father had been saying to Adam when she'd walked into his studio the night after the Titian switch? Something... Something... about involving her figuratively.

"Root rot," she muttered and squeezed her eyes shut in concentration. "What the devil was that supposed to mean?" Just as she was about to give up, the idea seeped in. Her eyes sprang open as she sprang up. "It'd be just like him!"

Grabbing a robe, she dashed from the room.

For a moment in the hall she hesitated. Perhaps she should wake Adam and tell him of her theory. Then again, it was no more than that, and he hadn't had the easier day of it either. If she produced results, then she'd wake him. And if she were wrong, her father would kill her.

She made a quick trip to her father's studio, then went down to the dining room.

On neither trip did she bother with lights. She wanted no one to pop out of their room and ask what she was up to. Carrying a rag, a bottle and a stack of newspapers, she went silently through the dark. Once she'd reached the dining room, she turned on the lights. No one would investigate downstairs except Cards. He'd never question her. She worked quickly.

Kirby spread the newspapers in thick pads on the dining room table. Setting the bottle and the rag on them, she turned to her own portrait.

"You're too clever for your own good, Papa," she murmured as she studied the painting. "I'd never be able to tell if this was a duplicate. There's only one way."

Once she'd taken the portrait from the wall, Kirby laid it on the newspaper. "It's value goes below the surface," she murmured. Isn't that what he'd said to Harriet? And he'd been smug. He'd been smug right from the start. Kirby opened the bottle and tipped the liquid onto the rag. "Forgive me, Papa," she said quietly.

With the lightest touch—an expert's touch—she began to remove layers of paint in the lower corner. Minutes passed. If she were wrong, she wanted the damage to be minimal. If she were right, she had something priceless in her hands. Either way, she couldn't rush.

She dampened the rag and wiped again. Her father's bold signature disappeared, then the bright summer grass beneath it, and the primer.

And there, beneath where there should have been only canvas, was a dark, somber brown. One letter, then another appeared. It was all that was necessary.

"Great buckets of blood," she murmured. "I was right."

Beneath the feet of the girl she'd been was Rembrandt's signature. She'd go no further. As carefully as she'd unstopped it, Kirby secured the lid of the bottle.

"So, Papa, you put Rembrandt to sleep under a copy of my portrait. Only you would've thought to copy yourself to pull it off."

"Very clever."

Whirling, Kirby looked behind her into the dark outside the dining room. She knew the voice; it didn't frighten her. As her heart pounded, the shadows moved. What now, she asked herself quickly. Just how would she explain it?

"Cleverness runs in the family, doesn't it, Kirby?"

"So I'm told." She tried to smile. "I'd like to explain. You'd better come in out of the dark and sit down. It could take—" She stopped as the first part of the invitation was accepted. She stared at the barrel of a small polished revolver. Lifting her gaze from it, she stared into clear, delicate blue eyes. "Melly, what's going on?"

"You look surprised. I'm glad." With a satisfied smile, Melanie aimed the gun at Kirby's head. "Maybe you're not so clever after all."

"Don't point that at me."

"I intend to point it at you." She lowered the gun to chest level. "And I'll do more than point it if you move."

"Melly." She wasn't afraid, not yet. She was confused, even annoyed, but she wasn't afraid of the woman she'd grown up with. "Put that thing away and sit down. What're you doing here this time of night?"

"Two reasons. First, to see if I could find any trace of the painting you've so conveniently found for me.

Second, to finish the job that was unsuccessful this morning."

"This morning?" Kirby took a step forward then froze as she heard the quick, deadly click. Good God, could it actually be loaded? "Melly..."

"I suppose I must have miscalculated a bit or you'd be dead already." The elegant rose silk whispered as she shrugged. "I know the passages very well. Remember, you used to drag me around in them when we were children—before you went in with a faulty flashlight. I'd changed the batteries in it, you see. I'd never told you about that, had I?" She laughed as Kirby remained silent. "I used the passages this morning. Once I was sure you and Adam were settled in, I went out and turned on the gas by the main valve—I'd already broken the switch on the unit."

"You can't be serious." Kirby dragged a hand through her hair.

"Deadly serious, Kirby."

"Why?"

"Primarily for money, of course."

"Money?" She would've laughed, but her throat was closing. "But you don't need money."

"You're so smug." The venom came through. Kirby wondered that she'd never heard it before. "Yes, I need money."

"You wouldn't take a settlement from your ex-husband."

"He wouldn't give me a dime," Melanie corrected. "He cut me off, and as he had me cold on adultery, I wasn't in a position to take him to court. He let me get a quiet, discreet divorce so that our reputations wouldn't suffer. And except for one incident, I'd been very discreet. Stuart and I were always very careful."

"Stuart?" Kirby lifted a hand to rub at her temple. "You and Stuart?"

"We've been lovers for over three years. Questions are just buzzing around in your head, aren't they?" Enjoying herself, Melanie stepped closer. The whiff of Chanel followed her. "It was more practical for us if we pretended to be just acquaintances. I convinced Stuart to ask you to marry him. My inheritance has dwindled to next to nothing. Your money would have met Stuart's and my tastes very nicely. And we'd have got close to Uncle Philip."

She ignored the rest and honed in on the most important. "What do you want from my father?"

"I found out about the little game he and mother indulged in years ago. Not all the details, but enough to know I could use it if I had to. I thought it was time to use your father's talent for my own benefit."

"You made plans to steal from your own mother."

"Don't be so self-righteous." Her voice chilled. The gun was steady. "Your father betrayed her without a murmur then double-crossed us in the bargain. Now you've solved that little problem for me." With her free hand, she gestured to the painting. "I should be grateful I failed this morning. I'd still be looking for the painting."

Somehow, some way, she'd deal with this. Kirby started with the basics. "Melly, how could you hurt me? We've been friends all our lives."

"Friends?" The word sounded like an obscenity. "I've hated you for as long as I can remember."

"No—"

"Hated," Melanie repeated, coldly this time and with the ring of truth. "It was always you people flocked around, always you men preferred. My own mother preferred you."

"That's not true." Did it go so deep? Kirby thought with a flood of guilt. Should she have seen it before? "Melly—" But as she started forward, Melanie gestured with the gun.

"Melanie, don't be so stiff and formal.... Melanie, where's your sense of humor?" Her eyes narrowed into slits. "She never came right out and said I should be more like you, but that's what she wanted."

"Harriet loves you—"

"Love?" Melanie cut Kirby off with a laugh. "I don't give a damn for love. It won't buy what I need. You may have taken my mother, but that was a minor offense. The men you snatched from under my nose time and time again is a bigger one."

"I never took a man from you. I've never shown an interest in anyone you were serious about."

"There have been dozens," Melanie corrected. Her voice was as brittle as glass. "You'd smile and say something stupid and I'd be forgotten. You never had my looks, but you'd use that so-called charm and lure them away, or you'd freeze up and do the same thing."

"I might've been friendly to someone you cared for," Kirby said quickly. "If I froze it was to discourage them. Good God, Melly, I'd never have done anything to hurt you. I love you."

"I've no use for your love any longer. It served its purpose well enough." She smiled slowly as tears swam in Kirby's eyes. "My only regret is that you didn't fall for Stuart. I wanted to see you fawn over him, knowing he preferred me—married you only because I wanted it. When you came to see him that night, I nearly came out of the bedroom just for the pleasure of seeing your face. But..." She shrugged. "We had long-range plans."

"You used me," Kirby said quietly when she could no longer deny it. "You had Stuart use me."

"Of course. Still, it wasn't wise of me to come back from New York for the weekend to be with him."

"Why, Melanie? Why have you pretended all these years?"

"You were useful. Even as a child I knew that. Later, in Paris, you opened doors for me, then again in New York. It was even due to you that I spent a year of luxury with Carlyse. You wouldn't sleep with him and you wouldn't marry him. I did both."

"And that's all?" Kirby murmured. "That's all?"

"That's all. You're not useful any longer, Kirby. In fact, you're an inconvenience. I'd planned your death as a warning to Uncle Philip, now it's just a necessity."

She wanted to turn away, but she needed to face it. "How could I have known you all my life and not seen it? How could you have hated me and not shown it?"

"You let emotions rule your life, I don't. Pick up the painting, Kirby." With the gun, she gestured. "And be careful with it. Stuart and I have been offered a healthy sum for it. If you call out," she added, "I'll shoot you now and be in the passage with the painting before anyone comes down."

"What are you going to do?"

"We're going into the passage. You're going to have a nasty spill, Kirby, and break your neck. I'm going to take the painting home and wait for the call to tell me of your accident.''

She'd stall. If only she'd woken Adam... No, if she'd woken him, he, too, would have a gun pointed at him. "Everyone knows how I feel about the passages.''

"It'll be a mystery. When they find the empty space on the wall, they'll know the Rembrandt was responsible. Stuart should be the first target, but he's out of town and has been for three days. I'll be devastated by the death of my oldest and dearest friend. It'll take months in Europe to recover from the grief.''

"You've thought this out carefully.'' Kirby rested against the table. "But are you capable of murder, Melly?'' Slowly she closed her fingers around the bottle, working off the top with her thumb. "Face to face murder, not remote control like this morning.''

"Oh, yes.'' Melanie smiled, beautifully. "I prefer it. I feel better with you knowing who's going to kill you. Now pick up the painting, Kirby. It's time.''

With a jerk of her arm, Kirby tossed the turpentine mixture, splattering it on Melanie's neck and dress. When Melanie tossed up her hand in protection, Kirby lunged. Together they fell in a rolling heap onto the floor, the gun pressed between them.

"What do you mean Hiller's been in New York since yesterday?'' Adam demanded. "What happened this morning wasn't an accident. He had to have done it.''

"No way.'' In a few words McIntyre broke Adam's theory. "I have a good man on him. I can give you the name of Hiller's hotel. I can give you the name of the restaurant where he had lunch and what he ate while you were throwing chairs through windows. He's got his alibi cold, Adam, but it doesn't mean he didn't arrange it."

"Damn." Adam lowered the transmitter while he rearranged his thinking. "It gives me a bad feeling, Mac. Dealing with Hiller's one thing, but it's a whole new story if he has a partner or he's hired a pro to do his dirty work. Kirby needs protection, official protection. I want her out."

"I'll work on it. The Rembrandt—"

"I don't give a damn about the Rembrandt," Adam tossed back. "But it'll be in my hands tomorrow if I have to hang Fairchild up by his thumbs."

McIntyre let out a sigh of relief. "That's better. You were making me nervous thinking you were hung up on the Fairchild woman."

"I am hung up on the Fairchild woman," Adam returned mildly. "So you'd better arrange for—" He heard the shot. One, sharp and clean. It echoed and echoed through his head. "*Kirby!*" He thought of nothing else as he dropped the open transmitter on the floor and ran.

He called her name again as he raced downstairs. But his only answer was silence. He called as he rushed like a madman through the maze of rooms downstairs, but she didn't call back. Nearly blind with terror, his own voice echoing back to mock him, he ran on, slamming on lights as he went until the house was lit up like a celebration. Racing headlong into the dining room, he nearly fell over the two figures on the floor.

"Oh, my God!"

"I've killed her! Oh, God, Adam, help me! I think I've killed her!" With tears streaming down her face, Kirby pressed a blood-soaked linen napkin against Melanie's side. The stain spread over the rose silk of the dress and onto Kirby's hand.

"Keep the pressure firm." He didn't ask questions but grabbed a handful of linen from the buffet behind him. Nudging Kirby aside, he felt for a pulse. "She's alive." He pressed more linen to Melanie's side. "Kirby—"

Before he could speak again, there was chaos. The rest of the household poured into the dining room from every direction. Polly let out one squeal that never ended.

"Call an ambulance," Adam ordered Cards even as the butler turned to do so. "Shut her up, or get her out," he told Rick, nodding to Polly.

Recovering quickly, Fairchild knelt beside his daughter and the daughter of his closest friend. "Kirby, what happened here?"

"I tried to take the gun from her." She struggled to breathe as she looked down at the blood on her hands. "We fell. I don't—Papa, I don't even know which one of us pulled the trigger. Oh, God, I don't even know."

"Melanie had a gun?" Steady as a rock, Fairchild took Kirby's shoulders and turned her to face him. "Why?"

"She hates me." Her voice shook, then leveled as she stared into her father's face. "She's always hated me, I never knew. It was the Rembrandt, Papa. She'd planned it all."

"Melanie?" Fairchild glanced beyond Kirby to the unconscious figure on the floor. "She was behind it." He fell silent, only a moment. "How bad, Adam?"

"I don't know, damn it. I'm an artist not a doctor." There was fury in his eyes and blood on his hands. "It might've been Kirby."

"Yes, you're right." Fairchild's fingers tightened on his daughter's shoulder. "You're right."

"I found the Rembrandt," Kirby murmured. If it was shock that was making her light-headed, she wouldn't give in to it. She forced herself to think and to speak clearly.

Fairchild looked at the empty space on the wall, then at the table where the painting lay. "So you did."

With a cluck of her tongue, Tulip pushed Fairchild aside and took Kirby by the arm. Ignoring everyone else, she pulled Kirby to her feet. "Come with me, lovie. Come along with me now, that's a girl."

Feeling helpless, Adam watched Kirby being led away while he fought to stop the bleeding. "You'd better have a damn good explanation," he said between his teeth as his gaze swept over Fairchild.

"Explanations don't seem to be enough at this point," he murmured. Very slowly he rose. The sound of sirens cut through the quiet. "I'll phone Harriet."

Almost an hour had passed before Adam could wash the blood from his hands. Unconscious still, Melanie was speeding on her way to the hospital. His only thought was for Kirby now, and he left his room to find her. When he reached the bottom landing, he came upon an argument in full gear. Though the shouting was all one-sided, the noise vibrated through the hall.

"I want to see Adam Haines and I want to see him immediately!"

"Gate crashing, Mac?" Adam moved forward to stand beside Cards.

"Adam, thank God." The small, husky man with a squared-off face and disarming eyes ran a hand through his disheveled mat of hair. "I didn't know what'd happened to you. Tell this wall to move aside, will you?"

"It's all right, Cards." He drew an expressionless stare. "He's not a reporter. I know him."

"Very well, sir."

"What the hell's going on?" McIntyre demanded when Cards walked back down the hall. "Who just got carted out of here in an ambulance? Damn it, Adam, I thought it might be you. Last thing I know, you're shouting and breaking transmission."

"It's been a rough night." Putting a hand on his shoulder, Adam led him into the parlor. "I need a drink." Going directly to the bar, Adam poured, drank and poured again. "Drink up, Mac," he invited. "This has to be better than the stuff you've been buying in that little motel down the road. Philip," he continued as Fairchild walked into the room, "I imagine you could use one of these."

"Yes." With a nod of acknowledgment for McIntyre, and no questions, Fairchild accepted the glass Adam offered.

"We'd better sit down. Philip Fairchild," Adam went on as Fairchild settled himself, "Henry McIntyre, investigator for the Commonwealth Insurance company."

"Ah, Mr. McIntyre." Fairchild drank half his scotch in one gulp. "We have quite a bit to discuss. But first, Adam, satisfy my curiosity. How did you become involved with the investigation?"

"It's not the first time I've worked for Mac, but it's the last." He sent McIntyre a quiet look that was lined in steel. "There's a matter of our being cousins," he added. "Second cousins."

"Relatives." Fairchild smiled knowingly, then gave McIntyre a charming smile.

"You knew why I was here," Adam said. "How?"

"Well, Adam, my boy, it's nothing to do with your cleverness." Fairchild tossed off the rest of the scotch then rose to fill his glass again. "I was expecting someone to come along. You were the only one who did." He sat back down with a sigh. "Simple as that."

"Expecting?"

"Would someone tell me who was in that ambulance?" McIntyre cut in.

"Melanie Burgess." Fairchild looked into his scotch. "Melly." It would hurt, he knew, for a long time. For himself, for Harriet and for Kirby. It was best to begin to deal with it. "She was shot when Kirby tried to take her gun away—the gun she was pointing at my daughter."

"Melanie Burgess," McIntyre mused. "It fits with the information I got today. Information," he added to Adam, "I was about to give you when you broke transmission. I'd like it from the beginning, Mr. Fairchild. I assume the police are on their way."

"Yes, no way around that." Fairchild sipped at his scotch and deliberated on just how to handle things.

Then he saw he no longer had McIntyre's attention. He was staring at the doorway.

Dressed in jeans and a white blouse, Kirby stood just inside the room. She was pale, but her eyes were dark. She was beautiful. It was the first thing McIntyre thought. The second was that she was a woman who could empty a man's mind the way a thirsty man empties a bottle.

"Kirby." Adam was up and across the room. He had his hands on hers. Hers were cold, but steady. "Are you all right?"

"Yes. Melanie?"

"The paramedics handled everything. I got the impression the wound wasn't as bad as it looked. Go lie down," he murmured. "Forget it for a while."

"No." She shook her head and managed a weak smile. "I'm fine really. I've been washed and patted and plied with liquor, though I wouldn't mind another. The police will want to question me." Her gaze drifted to McIntyre. She didn't ask, but simply assumed he was with the police. "Do you need to talk to me?"

It wasn't until then he realized he'd been staring. Clearing his throat, McIntyre rose. "I'd like to hear your father's story first, Miss Fairchild."

"Wouldn't we all?" Struggling to find some balance, she walked to her father's chair. "Are you going to come clean, Papa, or should I hire a shady lawyer?"

"Unnecessary, my sweet." He took her hand and held it. "The beginning," he continued with a smile for McIntyre. "It started, I suppose, a few days before Harriet flew off to Africa. She's an absent-minded woman. She had to return to the gallery one night to pick up some papers she'd forgotten. When she saw the light in Stuart's office, she started to go in and scold him for working late. Instead she eavesdropped on his phone conversation and learned of his plans to steal the Rembrandt. Absent-minded but shrewd, Harriet left and let Stuart think his plans were undetected." He grinned and squeezed Kirby's hand. "An intelligent woman, she came directly to a friend known for his loyalty and his sharp mind."

"Papa." With a laugh of relief, she bent over and kissed his head. "You were working together, I should've known."

"We developed a plan. Perhaps unwisely, we decided not to bring Kirby into it." He looked up at her. "Should I apologize?"

"Never."

But the fingers brushing over her hand said it for him. "Kirby's relationship with Stuart helped us along in that decision. And her occasional short-sightedness. That is, when she doesn't agree with my point of view."

"I might take the apology after all."

"In any case." Rising, Fairchild began to wander around the room, hands clasped behind his back. His version of Sherlock Holmes, Kirby decided and settled back for the show. "Harriet and I both knew Stuart wasn't capable of constructing and carrying through on a theft like this alone. Harriet hadn't any idea whom he'd been talking to on the phone, but my name had been mentioned. Stuart had said he'd, ah, 'feel me out on the subject of producing a copy of the painting.'" His face fell easily into annoyed lines.

"I've no idea why he should've thought a man like me would do something so base, so dishonest."

"Incredible," Adam murmured and earned a blinding smile from father and daughter.

"We decided I'd agree, after some fee haggling. I'd then have the original in my possession while palming the copy off on Stuart. Sooner or later, his accomplice would be forced into the open to try to recover it. Meanwhile, Harriet reported the theft, but refused to file a claim. Instead she demanded that the insurance company act with discretion. Reluctantly she told them of her suspicion that I was involved, thereby ensuring that the investigation would be centered around me, and by association, Stuart and his accomplice. I concealed the Rembrandt behind a copy of a painting of my daughter, the original of which is tucked away in my room. I'm sentimental."

"Why didn't Mrs. Merrick just tell the police and the insurance company the truth?" McIntyre demanded after he'd worked his way through the explanation.

"They might have been hasty. No offense," Fairchild added indulgently. "Stuart might've been caught, but his accomplice would probably have gotten away. And, I confess, it was the intrigue that appealed to both of us. It was irresistible. You'll want to corroborate my story, of course."

"Of course," McIntyre agreed and wondered if he could deal with another loony.

"We'd have done things differently if we'd had any idea that Melanie was involved. It's going to be difficult for Harriet." Pausing, he aimed a long look at McIntyre that was abruptly no nonsense. "Be careful with her. Very careful. You might find our methods unorthodox, but she's a mother who's had two unspeakable shocks tonight: her daughter's betrayal and the possibility of losing her only child." He ran a hand over Kirby's hair as he stopped by her. "No matter how deep the hurt, the love remains, doesn't it, Kirby?"

"All I feel is the void," she murmured. "She hated me, and I think, I really think she wanted me dead more than she wanted the painting. I wonder...I wonder just how much I'm to blame for that."

"You can't blame yourself for being, Kirby." Fairchild cupped her chin. "You can't blame a tree for reaching for the sun or another for rotting from within. We make our own choices and we're each responsible for them. Blame and credit belong to the individual. You haven't the right to claim either from someone else."

"You won't let me cover the hurt with guilt." After a long breath she rose and kissed his cheek. "I'll have to deal with it." Without thinking she held out a hand for Adam before she turned to McIntyre. "Do you need a statement from me?"

"No, the shooting's not my jurisdiction, Miss Fairchild. Just the Rembrandt." Finishing off the rest of his scotch he rose. "I'll have to take it with me, Mr. Fairchild."

All graciousness, Fairchild spread his arms wide. "Perfectly understandable."

"I appreciate your cooperation." If he could call it that. With a weary smile, he turned to Adam. "Don't worry, I haven't forgotten your terms. If everything's as he says, I should be able to keep them out of it officially, as we agreed the other day. Your part of the job's over, and all in all you handled it well. So, I'll be sorry if you're serious about not working for me any more. You got the Rembrandt back, Adam. Now I've got to get started on untangling the red tape.''

"Job?" Going cold, Kirby turned. Her hand was still linked in Adam's but she felt it go numb as she drew it slowly away. "Job?" she repeated, pressing the hand to her stomach as if to ward off a blow.

Not now, he thought in frustration and searched for the words he'd have used only a few hours later. "Kirby—"

With all the strength she had left, all the bitterness she'd felt, she brought her hand across his face. "Bastard," she whispered. She fled at a dead run.

"Damn you, Mac." Adam raced after her.

Chapter 12

Adam caught up to her just as Kirby started to slam her bedroom door. Shoving it open, he pushed his way inside. For a moment, they only stared at each other.

"Kirby, let me explain."

"No." The wounded look had been replaced by glacial anger. "Just get out. All the way out, Adam— of my house and my life."

"I can't." He took her by the shoulders, but her head snapped up and the look was so cold, so hard, he dropped his hands again. It was too late to explain the way he'd planned. Too late to prevent the hurt. Now he had to find the way around it. "Kirby, I know what you must be thinking. I want—"

"Do you?" It took all of her effort to keep her voice from rising. Instead it was cool and calm. "I'm going to tell you anyway so we can leave everything neat and tidy." She faced him because she refused to turn her back on the pain or on the betrayal. "I'm thinking that I've never detested anyone more than I detest you at this moment. I'm thinking Stuart and Melanie could take lessons on using people from you. I'm thinking how naive I was, how stupid to have believed there was something special about you, something stable and honest. And I wonder how I could've made love with you and never seen it. Then again, I didn't see it in Melanie, either. I loved and trusted her." Tears burned behind her eyes but she ignored them. "I loved and trusted you."

"Kirby..."

"Don't touch me." She backed away, but it was the tremor in her voice, not the movement that stopped him from going to her. "I don't ever want to feel your hands on me again." Because she wanted to weep, she laughed, and the sound was as sharp as a knife. "I've always admired a really good liar, Adam, but you're the best. Every time you touched me, you lied. You prostituted yourself in that bed." She gestured toward it and wanted to scream. She wanted to fling herself on it and weep until she was empty. She stood, straight as an arrow. "You lay beside me and said all the things I wanted to hear. Do you get extra points for that, Adam? Surely that was above and beyond the call of duty."

"Don't." He'd had enough. Enough of her cold, clear look, her cold, clear words. "You know there was no dishonesty there. What happened between us had nothing to do with the rest."

"It has everything to do with it."

"No." He'd take everything else she could fling at him, but not that. She'd changed his life with hardly more than a look. She had to know it. "I should never have put my hands on you, but I couldn't stop myself. I wanted you. I needed you. You have to believe that."

"I'll tell you what I believe," she said quietly because every word he spoke was another slice into her heart. She'd finished with being used. "You came here for the Rembrandt, and you meant to find it no matter who or what you had to go through. My father and I were means to an end. Nothing more, nothing less."

He had to take it, had to let her say it, but there'd be no lies between them any longer. "I came for the Rembrandt. When I walked through the door I only had one priority, to find it. But I didn't know you when I walked through the door. I wasn't in love with you then."

"Is this the part where you say everything changed?" she demanded, falling back on fury. "Shall we wait for the violins?" She was weakening. She turned away and leaned on the post of the bed. "Do better, Adam."

She could be cruel. He remembered her father's warning. He only wished he believed he had a defense. "I can't do better than the truth."

"Truth? What the hell do you know about truth?" She whirled back around, eyes damp now and shimmering with heat. "I stood here in this room and told you everything, everything I knew about my father. I trusted you with his welfare, the most important thing in my life. Where was your truth then?"

"I had a commitment. Do you think it was easy for me to sit here and listen, knowing I couldn't give you what you were giving me?"

"Yes." Her tone was dead calm, her eyes fierce. "Yes, I think it was a matter of routine for you. If you'd told me that night, the next day or the next, I might've believed you. If I'd heard it from you, I might've forgiven you."

Timing. Hadn't she told him how vital timing could be? Now he felt her slipping away from him but he had nothing but excuses to give her. "I was going to tell you everything, start to finish, tomorrow."

"Tomorrow?" Slowly she nodded. "Tomorrows are very convenient. A pity for us all how rarely they come."

All the warmth, all the fire that had drawn him to her was gone. He'd only seen this look on her face once before—when Stuart had backed her into a corner and she'd had no escape. Stuart had used physical dominance, but it was no prettier than the emotional pressure Adam knew he used. "I'm sorry, Kirby. If I'd taken the risk and told you this morning, it would've been different for all of us."

"I don't want your apology!" The tears beat her and poured out. She'd sacrificed everything else, now her pride was gone as well. "I thought I'd found the man I could share my life with. I fell in love with you in the flash of an instant. No questions, no doubts. I believed everything you said to me. I gave you everything I had. In all my life no one's been allowed to know me as you did. I entrusted you with everything I am and you used me." Turning, she pressed her face into the bedpost.

He had, he couldn't deny it even to himself. He'd used her, as Stuart had used her. As Melanie had used her. Loving her made no difference, yet he had to hope it made all the difference. "Kirby." It took all the strength he had not to go to her, to comfort her, but he'd only be comforting himself if he put his arms around her now. "There's nothing you can say to me I haven't said to myself. I came here to do a job but I fell in love with you. There wasn't any warning for me, either. I know I've hurt you. There's nothing I can do to turn back the clock."

"Do you expect me to fall into your arms? Do you expect me to say nothing else matters but us?" She turned and though her cheeks were still damp, her eyes were dry. "It all matters," she said flatly. "Your job's finished here, Adam. You've recovered your Rembrandt. Take it, you earned it."

"You're not going to cut me out of your life."

"You've done that for me."

"No." The fury and frustration took over so that he grabbed her arm and jerked her against him. "No, you'll have to adjust to the way things are because I'm coming back." He ran his hands down her hair and they weren't steady. "You can make me suffer. By God, you can do it. I'll give you that, Kirby, but I'll be back."

Before his anger could push him too far, he whirled around and left her alone.

Fairchild was waiting for him, sitting calmly in the parlor by the fire. "I thought you'd need this." Without getting up, he gestured to the glass of scotch on the table beside him. He waited until Adam had tossed it back. He didn't need to be told what had passed between them. "I'm sorry. She's hurt. Perhaps in time the wounds will close and she'll be able to listen."

Adam's knuckles whitened on the glass. "That's what I told her, but I didn't believe it. I betrayed her." His glance lowered and settled on the older man. "And you."

"You did what you had to do. You had a part to play." Fairchild spread his hands on his knees and stared at them, thinking of his own part. "She would've dealt with it, Adam. She's strong enough. But even Kirby has a breaking point. Melanie... It was too soon after Melanie."

"She won't let me comfort her." It was that anguish that had him turning to stare out of the window. "She looks so wounded, and my being here only makes it harder for her." Steadying himself, he stared out at nothing. "I'll be out as soon as I can pack." He turned, his head only, and looked at the small, balding man in front of the fire. "I love her, Philip."

In silence Fairchild watched Adam walk away. For the first time in his six decades he felt old. Old and tired. With a deep, deep sigh he rose and went to his daughter.

He found her curled on her bed, her head cradled by her knees and arms. She sat silent and unmoving and he knew, utterly, utterly beaten. When he sat beside her, her head jerked up. Slowly, with his hand stroking her hair, her muscles relaxed.

"Do we ever stop making fools of ourselves, Papa?"

"You've never been a fool."

"Oh, yes, yes, it seems I have." Settling her chin on her knees she stared straight ahead. "I lost our bet. I guess you'll be breaking open that box of cigars you've been saving."

"I think we can consider the extenuating circumstances."

"How generous of you." She tried to smile and failed. "Aren't you going to the hospital to be with Harriet?"

"Yes, of course."

"You'd better go then. She needs you."

His thin, bony hand continued to stroke her hair. "Don't you?"

"Oh, Papa." Tears came in a flood as she turned into his arms.

Kirby followed Cards downstairs as he carried her bags. In the week since the discovery of the Rembrandt she'd found it impossible to settle. She found no comfort in her art, no comfort in her home. Everything here held memories she could no longer deal with. She slept little and ate less. She knew she was losing touch with the person she was, and so she'd made plans to force herself back.

She opened the door for Cards and stared out at the bright, cheery morning. It made her want to weep.

"I don't know why a sensible person would get up at this ridiculous hour to drive to the wilderness."

Kirby forced back the gloom and turned to watch her father stride down the stairs in a ratty bathrobe and bare feet. What hair he had left was standing on end. "The early bird gathers no moss," she told him. "I want to get to the lodge and settle in. Want some coffee?"

"Not while I'm sleeping," he muttered as she nuzzled his cheek. "I don't know what's wrong with you, going off to that shack in the Himalayas."

"It's Harriet's very comfortable cabin in the Adirondacks, twenty miles from Lake Placid."

"Don't nitpick. You'll be alone."

"I've been alone before," she reminded him. "You're annoyed because you won't have anyone but Cards to shout at for a few weeks."

"He never shouts back." But even as he grumbled, Fairchild was studying Kirby's face. The shadows were still under her eyes and the loss of weight was much too apparent. "Tulip should go with you. Someone has to make you eat."

"I'm going to do that. Mountain air should make me ravenous." When he continued to frown at her she touched his cheek. "Don't worry, Papa."

"I am worried." Taking her shoulders, he held her at arm's length. "For the first time in your life, you're causing me genuine concern."

"A few pounds, Papa."

"Kirby." He cupped her face in his strong thin hand. "You have to talk to Adam."

"No!" The word came out violently. With an effort she drew a steadying breath. "I've said all I want to say to Adam. I need time and some solitude, that's all."

"Running away, Kirby?"

"As fast as I can. Papa, Rick proposed to me again before he left."

"What the hell does that have to do with anything?" he demanded. "He always proposes to you before he leaves."

"I nearly said yes." She lifted her hands to his, willing him to understand. "I nearly said yes because it seemed an easy way out. I'd have ruined his life."

"What about yours?"

"I have to glue the pieces back together. Papa, I'll be fine. It's Harriet who needs you now."

He thought of his friend, his oldest and closest friend. He thought of the grief. "Melanie's going to Europe when she's fully recovered."

"I know." Kirby tried not to remember the gun, or the hate. "Harriet told me. She'll need both of us when Melly's gone. If I can't help myself, how can I help Harriet?"

"Melanie won't see Harriet. The girl's destroying herself with hate." He looked at his own daughter, his pride, his treasure. "The sooner Melanie's out of the hospital and thousands of miles away, the better it'll be for everyone."

She knew what he'd done, how he'd fought against his feelings about Melanie to keep from causing either her or Harriet more grief. He'd comforted them both without releasing his own fury. She held him tightly a moment, saying nothing. Needing to say nothing.

"We all need some time," she murmured. When she drew away she was smiling. She wouldn't leave him with tears in her eyes. I'll cloister myself in the wilderness and sculpt while you pound on your hawk."

"Such a wicked tongue in such a pretty face."

"Papa..." Absently she checked the contents of her purse. "Whatever painting you do will be done under your own name?" When he didn't answer, she glanced up, narrowing her yes. "Papa?"

"All my paintings will be Fairchilds. Haven't I given you my word?" He sniffed and looked injured. Kirby began to feel alarmed.

"This obsession with sculpting," she began, eyeing him carefully. "You don't have it in your head to attempt an emulation of a Rodin or Cellini?"

"You ask too many questions," he complained as he nudged her toward the door. "The day's wasting away, better get started. Don't forget to write."

Kirby paused on the porch and turned back to him. "It'll take you years," she decided. "If you ever acquire the talent. Go ahead and play with your hawk." She kissed his forehead. "I love you, Papa."

He watched her dart down the steps and into her car. "One should never interfere in the life of one's child," he murmured. Smiling broadly, he waved goodbye. When she was out of sight, he went directly to the phone.

The forest had always appealed to her. In midautumn, it shouted with life. The burst of colors were a last swirling fling before the trees went into the final cycle. It was an order Kirby accepted—birth, growth, decay, rebirth. Still, after three days alone, she hadn't found her serenity.

The stream she walked past rushed and hissed. The air was brisk and tangy. She was miserable.

She'd nearly come to terms with her feelings about Melanie. Her childhood friend was ill, had been ill for a long, long time and might never fully recover. It hadn't been a betrayal any more than cancer was a betrayal. But it was a malignancy Kirby knew she had to cut out of her life. She'd nearly accepted it, for Melanie's sake and her own.

She could come to terms with Melanie, but she had yet to deal with Adam. He'd had no illness, nor a lifetime of resentments to feed it. He'd simply had a job to do. And that was too cold for her to accept.

With her hands in her pockets she sat down on a log and scowled into the water. Her life, she admitted, was a mess. She was a mess. And she was damn sick of it.

She tried to tell herself she'd put Adam out of her life. She hadn't. Yes, she'd refused to listen to him. She'd made no attempt to contact him. It wasn't enough. It wasn't enough, Kirby decided, because it left things unfinished. Now she'd never know if he'd had any real feelings for her. She'd never know if, even briefly, he'd belonged to her.

Perhaps it was best that way.

Standing, she began to walk again, scuffling the leaves that danced around her feet. She was tired of herself. Another first. It wasn't going to go on, she determined. Whatever the cost, she was going to whip Kirby Fairchild back into shape. Starting now. At a brisk pace, she started back to the cabin.

She liked the way it looked, set deep in the trees by itself. The roof was pitched high and the glass sparkled. Today, she thought as she went in through the back door, she'd work. After she'd worked, she'd eat until she couldn't move.

Peeling off her coat as she went, she walked directly to the work table she'd set up in the corner of the living room. Without looking around, she tossed the coat aside and looked at her equipment. She hadn't touched it in days. Now she sat and picked up a formless piece of wood. This was to be her *Passion*. Perhaps now more than ever, she needed to put that emotion into form.

There was silence as she explored the feel and life of the wood in her hands. She thought of Adam, of the nights, the touches, the tastes. It hurt. Passion could. Using it, she began to work.

An hour slipped by. She only noticed when her fingers cramped. With a sigh, she set the wood down and stretched them. The healing had begun. She could be certain of it now. "A start," she murmured to herself. "It's a start."

"It's *Passion*. I can already see it."

The knife slipped out of her hand and clattered on the table as she whirled. Across the room, calmly sitting in a faded wing-back chair, was Adam. She'd nearly sprung out of the chair to go to him before she stopped herself. He looked the same, just the same. But nothing was. That she had to remember.

"How did you get in here?"

He heard the ice in her voice. But he'd seen her eyes. In that one instant she'd told him everything he'd ached for. Still he knew she couldn't be rushed. "The front door wasn't locked." He rose and crossed to her. "I came inside to wait for you, but when you came in, you looked so intense; then you started right in. I didn't want to disturb your work." When she said nothing, he picked up the wood and turned it over in his hand. He thought it smoldered. "Amazing," he murmured. "Amazing what power you have." Just holding it made him want her more, made him want what she'd put into the wood. Carefully he set it down again, but his eyes were just as intense when he studied her. "What the hell've you been doing? Starving yourself?"

"Don't be ridiculous." She stood and walked away from him, but she didn't know where to go.

"Am I to blame for that, too?"

His voice was quiet, serious. She'd never be able to resist that tone. Gathering her strength, she turned back to him. "Did Tulip send you to check up on me?"

She was too thin. Damn it. Had the pounds melted off her? She was so small. How could she be so small and look so arrogant? He wanted to go to her. Beg. He was nearly certain she'd listen now. Yet she wouldn't want it that way. Instead he tucked his hands in his pockets and rocked back on his heels. "This is a cozy little place. I wandered around a bit while you were out."

"Glad you made yourself at home."

"It's everything Harriet said it would be." He looked at her again and smiled. "Isolated, cozy, charming."

She lifted a brow. It was easiest with the distance between them. "You've spoken to Harriet?"

"I took your portrait to the gallery."

Emotion came and went again her eyes. Picking up a small brass pelican, she caressed it absently. "My portrait?"

"I promised her she could exhibit it when I'd finished." He watched her nervous fingers run over the brass. "It wasn't difficult to finish without you. I saw you everywhere I looked."

Quickly she turned to walk to the front wall. It was all glass, open to the woods. No one could feel trapped with that view. Kirby clung to it. "Harriet's having a difficult time."

"The strain shows a bit." In her, he thought, and in you. "I think it's better for her that Melanie won't see her at this point. With Stuart out of the way, the gallery's keeping Harriet busy." He stared at her back, trying to imagine what expression he'd find on her face. "Why aren't you pressing charges, Kirby?"

"For what purpose?" she countered. She set the piece of brass down. A crutch was a crutch and she was through with them. "Both Stuart and Melanie are disgraced, banished from the elite that means so much to them. The publicity's been horrid. They have no money, no reputation. Isn't that punishment enough?"

"Melanie tried to kill you. Twice." Suddenly furious by the calm, even tone, he went to her and spun her around. "Damn it, Kirby, she wanted you dead!"

"It was she who nearly died." Her voice was still even, but she took a step back from him. "The police have to accept my story that the gun went off accidentally, even if others don't. I could have sent Melly to jail. Wouldn't I feel avenged watching Harriet suffer?"

Adam forced back the impatience and stared through the glass. "She's worried about you."

"Harriet?" Kirby shrugged. "There's no need. When you see her, tell her I'm well."

"You can tell her yourself when we get back."

"We?" The lightest hint of temper entered her voice. Nothing could have relieved him more. "I'm going to be here for some time yet."

"Fine. I've nothing better to do."

"That wasn't an invitation."

"Harriet already gave me one," he told her easily. He gave the room another sweeping glance while Kirby smoldered. "The place looks big enough for two."

"That's where you're wrong, but don't let me spoil your plans." She spun on her heel and headed for the stairs. Before she'd gotten five feet, his fingers curled around her arm and held her still. When she whirled, he saw that his gypsy was back.

"You don't really think I'd let you leave? Kirby, you disappoint me."

"You don't *let* me do anything, Adam. Nor do you prevent me from doing anything."

"Only when it's necessary." While she stood rigid, he put his hands on her shoulders. "You're going to listen to me this time. And you're going to start listening in just a minute."

He pressed his mouth to hers as he'd needed to for weeks. She didn't resist. Nor did she respond. He could feel her fighting the need to do both. He could press her, he knew, and she'd give in to him. Then he might never really have her. Slowly their gazes locked; he straightened.

"You're nearly through making me suffer," he murmured. "I've paid, Kirby, in every moment I haven't been with you. Through every night you haven't been beside me. When are you going to stop punishing me?"

"I don't want to punish you." It was true. She'd already forgiven him. Yet, her confidence, that strong, thin shield she'd always had, had suffered an enormous blow. This time when she stepped back he didn't try to stop her. "I know we parted badly. Maybe it'd be best if we just admitted we'd both made a mistake

and left it at that. I realize you did what you had to do.
I've always done the same. It's time I got on with my
life and you with yours.''

He felt a quick jiggle of panic. She was too calm,
much too calm. He wanted emotion from her, any
kind she'd give. ''What sort of life would either of us
have without the other?''

None. But she shook her head. ''I said we made a
mistake—''

''And now you're going to tell me you don't love
me?''

She looked straight at him and opened her mouth.
Weakening, she shifted her gaze to just over his
shoulder. ''No, I don't love you, Adam. I'm sorry.''

She'd nearly cut him off at the knees. If she hadn't
looked away at the last instant, it would've been over
for him. ''I'd've thought you could lie better than
that.'' In one move he closed the distance between
them. His arms were around her, firm, secure. The
same, she thought. Nothing had changed after all.
''I've given you two weeks, Kirby. Maybe I should give
you more time, but I can't.'' He buried his face in her
hair while she squeezed her eyes shut. She'd been
wrong, she remembered. She'd been wrong about so
many things. Could this be right?

''Adam, please . . .''

''No, no more. I love you.'' He drew her away,
barely resisting the need to shake her. ''I love you and
you'll have to get used to it. It isn't going to change.''

She curled her hand into a fist before she could
stroke his cheek. ''I think you're getting pompous
again.''

"Then you'll have to get used to that, too. Kirby..."
He framed her face with his hands. "How many ways
would you like me to apologize?"

"No." Shaking her head she moved away again. She
should be able to think, she warned herself. She had
to think. "I don't need apologies, Adam."

"You wouldn't," he murmured. Forgiveness would
come as easily to her as every other emotion. "Your
father and I had a long talk before I drove up here."

"Did you?" She gave her attention to a bowl of
dried flowers. "How nice."

"He's given me his word he'll no longer . . . emulate
paintings."

With her back to him she smiled. The pain vanished without her realizing it and with it, the doubts.
They loved. There was so little else in life. Still smiling, Kirby decided she wouldn't tell Adam of her father's ambition with sculpting. Not just yet. "I'm glad
you convinced him," she said with her tongue in her
cheek.

"He decided to concede the point to me, since I'm
going to be a member of the family."

With a flutter of her lashes, she turned. "How
lovely. Is Papa adopting you?"

"That wasn't precisely the relationship we dis-
cussed." Crossing to her, he took her into his arms
again. This time he felt the give and the strength. "Tell
me again that you don't love me."

"I don't love you," she murmured and pulled his
mouth to hers. "I don't want you to hold me." Her
arms wound around his neck. "I don't want you to
kiss me again. Now." Her lips clung to his, opening,
giving. As the heat built he groaned and drew her in.

"Obstinate, aren't you?" he muttered.

"Invariably."

"But are you going to marry me?"

"On my terms."

When her head tilted back, he ran kisses up the length of her throat. "Which are?"

"I may come easy, but I don't come free."

"What do you want, a marriage settlement?" On a half laugh, he drew her away. She was his, whoever, whatever she was. He'd never let her go again. "Can't you think of anything but money?"

"I'm fond of money—and we still have to discuss my sitting fee. However..." She drew a deep breath. "My terms for marriage are four children."

"Four?" Even knowing Kirby, he'd been caught off guard. "Four children?"

She moistened her lips but her voice was strong. "I'm firm on that number, Adam. The point's non-negotiable." Then her eyes were young and full of needs. "I want children. Your children."

Every time he thought he loved her completely, he found he could love her more. Still more. "Four?" he repeated with a slow nod. "Any preference to gender?"

The breath she'd been holding came out on a laugh. No, she hadn't been wrong. They loved. There was very little else. "I'm flexible, though a mix of some sort would be nice." She tossed her head back and smiled up at him. "What do you think?"

He swept her into his arms then headed for the stairs. "I think we'd better get started."

READERS' COMMENTS ON SILHOUETTE INTIMATE MOMENTS:

"About a month ago a friend loaned me my first Silhouette. I was thoroughly surprised as well as totally addicted. Last week I read a Silhouette Intimate Moments and I was even more pleased. They are the best romance series novels I have ever read. They give much more depth to the plot, characters, and the story is fundamentally realistic. They incorporate tasteful sex scenes, which is a must, especially in the 1980's. I only hope you can publish them fast enough."

S.B.*, Lees Summit, MO

"After noticing the attractive covers on the new line of Silhouette Intimate Moments, I decided to read the inside and discovered that this new line was more in the line of books that I like to read. I do want to say I enjoyed the books because they are so realistic and a lot more truthful than so many romance books today."

J.C., Onekama, MI

"I would like to compliment you on your books. I will continue to purchase all of the Silhouette Intimate Moments. They are your best line of books that I have had the pleasure of reading."

S.M., Billings, MT

*names available on request

Silhouette Intimate Moments

COMING NEXT MONTH

ABOVE AND BEYOND Erin St. Claire

Trevor had fought hard to win Kyla's love, but the future they could have together was jeopardized by the shadows of Trevor's past. He was not the stranger he seemed.

CASTLES IN THE SAND Lynda Trent

Diana was a businesswoman; she didn't have time for fun and games. But when she found herself stranded on an island with easygoing Joel Kennedy, she had no choice but to relax—and enjoy.

IMAGES Anna James

Tina hadn't wanted to return to modeling, but finances gave her no choice, and now that Adam Cole, head of Generation Cosmetics, had seen her, he wasn't going to let her go.

A VERY SPECIAL FAVOR Kristin James

Emily had been in love with her boss for ten years, thinking that he would never notice her. But now Emily was turning thirty, and Adam was going to make it a very special birthday.

AVAILABLE THIS MONTH:

MIDNIGHT RAINBOW
Linda Howard

PRICE ABOVE RUBIES
Mary Lynn Baxter

THE ART OF DECEPTION
Nora Roberts

THE di MEDICI BRIDE
Heather Graham Pozzessere